KILLING IN THE VILLAGE COMMONS

A VIKING WITCH MYSTERY

CATE MARTIN

Cover design by Shezaad Sudar.

Rune art by BettyStrange at Dreamstime.com.

Ratatoskr Press logo by Aidan Vincent Kise.

ISBN 978-1-951439-57-6

❀ Formatted with Vellum

CHAPTER ONE

I'M NOT sure whose idea it was to have my going away party after hours at Jessica's café. I don't remember ever even having a conversation about it. But when we found ourselves there after a long day of hiking along the area trails overlooking Lake Superior, it felt kind of perfect.

It was, after all, the exact place where I had met them all for the first time.

The lingering smells of coffee and pastries were very different from the beer and roasting meat aromas at my grandmother's meeting hall where we usually hung out.

The windows were facing the wrong way for a lake view, and anyway they were frosted over within minutes of the four of us breathing inside the building. But the near-constant sound of trucks roaring by, their headlights filling up the café even more brightly than the overhead lights, was a comfort.

This place, up by the freeway, was far more a part of the modern world than the fishing town of Runde in the river valley below us.

And the odds of coming across a direct descendant of the Viking Age were slimmer here as well, unless you included me in that number.

I wasn't sure if I should be counted as one of them yet. But that was part of why I was leaving my friends in the first place, and I buried those thoughts and feelings deep and summoned up a smile as we settled into the over-stuffed chairs that were grouped around the largest of the coffee tables.

"I know this little gathering is about saying farewell to Ingrid, but I want to get everyone's opinion on some stuff," Jessica said as she peeled off her pink beanie and stuffed it with her mittens into the pockets of her already-hanging coat before disappearing into the back room behind the counter of the café part of her bookstore café.

As hastily as she had ripped that hat off, her blonde braid-crown had been as perfect as when she'd first put that hat on hours before. I had no idea how she did that. My hair was in half-frozen snarls that would be knots even after the ice packed in it melted away.

"Too late for coffee. Should I make some tea? Something herbal?" Andrew offered, half moving towards the kettle beside the coffee machine behind the counter.

"No, I brought something better," Michelle said. She reached for a canvas bag she had left in the café that morning before our hike and pulled out a bottle of wine. "I thought a little change from mead and beer would be welcome."

"Oh, perfect!" Jessica said as she came back into the room with a tray in her hands. "I wanted you all to help me try these savory tarts and cheese biscuits. They'll go great with red wine."

"Did you bring glasses?" I asked, peeking into the top of the bag.

Michelle's face fell. "No. Just the corkscrew. I knew I was forgetting something."

"At least it wasn't the corkscrew," Andrew said as he opened the cupboard over the coffee machine and pulled out four mugs. "Cups we have."

"And pretensions we don't," I said as Michelle poured the wine into the mugs. We clinked them all together, then each took a sip. "That's nice."

"It's from a winery north of here," Michelle said.

"Isn't a little cold for wine here?" I asked.

"The grapes are from California, but they press the wine here," she told me.

"Interesting," I said, taking another sip. "I'm no connoisseur, but this is quite good."

"Try the food," Jessica said, even as she got back to her feet to run off again. But this time she didn't disappear in the back, rather she stopped at one of the computers, woke it up from sleep mode and started clicking through various windows.

"What are you doing?" Andrew asked her as he reached for one of the cheese biscuits. I took a tartlet and gave it an experimental sniff. Vegetables and cheese, for sure. I thought maybe leek and a sharp cheddar? I took a bite and added potato to that list. It was the perfect size; any bigger and it would be too rich to finish.

"I signed up for one of those music services so I can have something playing in the background, but I have like a zillion options and it's too overwhelming, so I've been putting off using it. Here," she said, clicking on something. Speakers I couldn't see filled the café with music. It was playing softly enough for a place of business, but the discordant sounds of guitars and drums were far too aggressive.

"No," Michelle said firmly.

"How about this?" Jessica said, clicking on something else. Now we had children singing a cover of a pop song. "No, never mind. This one?" she clicked again.

"I know that song," Andrew said after we'd all listened in silence for half a verse. "That's from the 80s, right? I can't place the band."

"It sounds Jazz Age to me," I said. "That torch song way of singing, you know what I mean?"

"Maybe it's a cover?" he said with a shrug and reached for another cheese biscuit. "It's a strong 'yes' vote for the biscuits from me, by the way," he said, holding a hand in front of his full mouth as he spoke.

"Oh, good," Jessica said, looking so relieved I only belatedly realized she had been nervous about what we were going to say.

"These tartlets are fantastic as well," I said. "Where did you find the recipe?"

"I combined a few different ones," she said. "I guess they're my own creation now. There's two kinds there, actually."

I looked at the tray and realized there were subtle differences. The ones closer to Michelle were lighter in color, but with darker green flecks. Broccoli, with a white cheddar, maybe?

"And the music?" she asked, hand still hovering over the mouse.

"Let's stick with this for a while," Andrew said. "It's kind of nice. Familiar, and yet not too familiar."

"Old stuff in a new way," Michelle said.

"Old stuff in an even older way," I said. "And yet the concept feels new. I like it."

Another lapse of silence fell over us. I told myself that the others were just focused on the wine and food, but I couldn't shake the feeling that my mentioning old and older things had just cast a pall over our little party.

Andrew took out his phone to glance at the screen before tucking it back away again. I shot him a questioning look, but he just shrugged. "I thought Luke would be here. Or, I mean, Loke."

"I'll be seeing plenty of him after today. Maybe he thought his presence would just remind us all of that," I said.

As if his presence could bring the party further down than mine was doing.

"It's not forever," Jessica reminded all of us. "Not that it will fly by or anything. But it's not forever. And any time you have something to add to your wall over there, you just have to send it to me through Loke."

I looked back over my shoulder at where a few carefully chosen examples of my art hung on the wall nearest the register. I had yet to sell anything, but the winter skiing season hadn't quite gotten under swing yet.

"I will," I said, although inside I was less sure I'd still have time for art. I was about to undertake a lot more responsibilities. And I only had the vaguest of ideas of what they would entail. If my grandmother knew what was being planned for my education, she wasn't sharing any of it with me.

Michelle clapped her hands together, making us all jump. "No more of this gloomy brooding. Finish up what's in your mugs. I brought two other wines to try, and we're getting through all of them before we say good night."

"And I have some homemade crackers for you all to try," Jessica said.

The next few hours were companionable, if far from outright happy. The wine and cheese were delicious, and Jessica's seeded crackers were amazing. When had she even baked these? We'd just spent the whole day together, the four of us.

But finally the last of the wine was gone, and we had gone from late night to very early morning.

"I should get going," I said.

"Yeah," Jessica said glumly. "You have that thing at dawn."

"Well, and the rest of you have normal jobs as well," I said. "You already closed the café for an entire day. You can't do that again tomorrow."

"No," she agreed. We all helped her clean up the mess we'd made, then pulled on hats and coats and mittens. The boots we'd left near the heater were dry and toasty-warm, although it didn't take more than a few steps out in the deep winter cold for that warmth to fade.

We trudged together in silence down the path to the road that ran along the lake shore. The night was clear with a million stars overhead, the nearly full moon gleaming brightly over the waters of Lake Superior.

"I guess this is where we part ways," Jessica said, pulling me into a tight hug. "Learn everything they have to teach you just as quick as you can."

"I will," I promised.

"Take care of you," Michelle said as she too gave me a hug so fierce I was grateful for the padding of my winter coat.

"I'll see you as soon as I can," I promised them both. Then I watched the two of them walking along the road to the north, to their respective childhood homes.

"Shall we?" Andrew said when their silhouettes were swallowed up by the shadows of the trees and the sounds of their boots over the snow lost under the rustling of waves on the shore.

"I guess so," I said, turning to the south.

It was only a few minutes' walk to his house. So short a way. Too short for everything I wanted to say.

But also too long, because this wasn't the time to say any of it. Aside from my own feelings being a tangled mess of confusion, even if I had sorted any of it out, what was there to say now? Now, when I'd be gone in the morning for months or maybe even years?

But Andrew didn't seem to mind my silence. We walked together beside the lake and looked up at the stars and said not a word. And it was kind of perfect.

"This is you?" I said when we reached his driveway.

"I'll walk the rest of the way with you," he said. "Have you set up your new place yet?"

"No, I haven't been back up to the village since I spoke with the council," I admitted. "But it's already furnished and everything. My grandmother's parents lived there until they died, and nothing has been moved since."

"No personal touches, then?" he asked.

"Well, my grandmother and I will be bringing up as much of my stuff as we can carry tomorrow," I said. "Not that I have all that much. You helped me unload my car when I got here to Runde, if you remember."

"Yeah, I remember," he said. He seemed to be thinking of something else, though.

"What is it?" I asked.

"Nothing," he said.

"It isn't nothing," I said.

"Okay, I just worry that you're not doing more to make the place really yours," he said.

"I will," I said. "I just wanted to spend every possible minute I had left in Runde being in Runde. Surely you understand?"

"I do," he said. "Perhaps it would be closer to the point if I just say that I worry. About you."

"I won't be in any danger," I said. I deliberately didn't mention Thorbjorn, who with his brothers was the chief reason I would never, ever be in any danger. But even in dark of night I could see in Andrew's eyes that he was thinking of Thorbjorn anyway.

"I know you'll be safe. I worry that you won't be *happy*," he said. "I know I don't know the first thing about what it means to be a volva, but I still worry you signed on to something much bigger than yourself."

"You don't think I can do it?" I asked, surprised to find myself hurt at the thought. I had taken his support for granted, I guess.

"No, that's not what I meant," he said with a frustrated sigh. "Just, maybe you're sacrificing too much and getting too little in return. That's what I meant."

"Okay," I said, but then shook my head. "No, I still don't follow you. What are you trying to tell me?"

"Never mind. It's probably not even my place to say. Just forget I said anything," he said.

We had reached the gate to my grandmother's back garden, and I undid the latch but didn't step inside. I could hear something scratching about in the snow-encrusted dried remains of her hedges and suspected my cat Mjolner had let himself outside again. You'd think cats would hate the cold, but Mjolner practically thrived on it.

"I don't want to forget," I told him. "Tell me what you're trying to say so I can hold on to the memory. Definitely don't leave me with this maddeningly awkward conversation as our last time together."

He took a deep breath but still seemed reluctant to speak again. I caught the sleeve of his parka in my mittened hand and pulled him a little closer.

"Tell me."

"Okay," he said, looking straight into my eyes. My stomach flipped over. It must have been a bit too much for him as well, as he quickly dropped his gaze.

"I like you," he said, speaking to my feet, or maybe even to his own. "I like you, who you are now. Not that I think you should never grow or change, of course. I just worry when you come back, maybe you won't be *you* anymore." He barked out a humorless laugh. "I know. Silly."

"It's not silly," I said. "To be honest, I worry about that too. I mean, my grandmother handles it all great, but I don't know if she isn't some kind of exception. The only other woman I know who had learned anything like what I'm going to start learning, she was really twisted. Maybe she started out that way. I think maybe she did? But what if she didn't? I don't have all the answers either."

He nodded, still looking down at the ground between us.

"Hey," I said, tugging his sleeve again. "I'm not going to forget you. And thank you for telling me what was weighing on you. I won't forget this moment either."

"And yourself," he said, finally looking at me again. "Don't forget yourself."

"I think it will be easier not to forget you," I said. I meant to say it lightly, like a little joke to dispel the moment. But somehow it came out of my throat all choked with sincerity.

And then his eyes were focused on my lips and he was leaning in, and my hand on his arm was gripping him way too tight.

This was a bad idea. I had specifically told myself before this last night with my friends that I wouldn't do anything that implied a future I couldn't promise any of them.

And now I was on the cusp of doing the very worst thing of all.

Yet I couldn't seem to stop it.

Then Andrew's face was moving away from mine so he could make eye contact, giving me a questioning look. But before I could answer, he cleared his throat and stepped away from me.

I was suddenly icy cold and hugged my arms around myself.

"Sorry," he said, clearing his throat again.

"*I'm* sorry," I said. "I just can't-"

But he held up a hand, cutting off the rest of my words. "I understand. I do. Best of luck to you. I mean it."

"Andrew," I said, but he just turned away and thrust his hands deep into his parka pockets as he walked back up the road to his own home.

I touched my mittened fingertips to my lips. I really wanted to chase him down, to turn him around and kiss him for all he was worth.

But it was still a really bad idea.

"Mew?" Mjolner chirped at me from somewhere inside the hedge.

"Yes, I'm all right," I said to him as I stepped into the garden and latched the gate behind me. "Come on. Let's go finish that packing."

I doubted very much I was ever going to get to sleep that night. Not with this heavy aching weight in my chest.

CHAPTER TWO

WHEN MY GRANDMOTHER came to my door just before dawn, I was still wide awake, just staring up at the wood panels over my bed, tucked in its cubby among an array of cupboards. She didn't knock, just waited for me to turn my head and give her a nod. She returned my nod, then headed back downstairs to the kitchen and the coffee I could just catch a whiff of in the air.

Mjolner wasn't there, hogging my pillow. I wondered if he had gone on ahead or was hunting in the garden.

He was planning to move up to Villmark with me, right?

I looked back up at the panels overhead. Just flat slats of oak, polished to a fine glow but otherwise unadorned. I was going to miss my little bed. And that feeling only intensified when I turned on my side to sneak one last look out at the view of Lake Superior framed by pine trees through the little window near my pillow.

Then I got up and got dressed and shoved the rest of my clothes into my duffel bag. I already had my art things packed and downstairs waiting by the door, so I followed the scent of coffee and fresh waffles down the stairs to the kitchen.

I set my things by the rack that held our walking sticks, then shuffled over to where my grandmother was holding out a large mug of coffee. But when I reached out for it, she moved it away, setting it on the table to pull me into a tight hug.

"Mormor," I said, surprised. "I'm still going to see you. This isn't goodbye."

"I know," she said, squeezing me all the tighter. "This is for you. You look a wreck."

"Gee, thanks," I said.

"I know you didn't sleep last night," she said. "Your poor heart."

"It's all right," I said as cheerily as I could. "Coffee would help."

"Of course," she said, finally letting me go. I reached for the mug and took a big swallow. The caffeine hit me at once in a rush. After a second swallow, I was ready to sit down at the table and turn my attention to the monster-sized waffle my grandmother had put in front of me. It was a savory waffle, filled with ham and cheese, and she drizzled a white sauce over the top of it before handing me a fork.

"I knew it was going to be a big day, but I had no idea it was going to be carb-loading big," I said. Then I took a bite and any other words I might have wanted to say were lost in a long hum of pleasure. The salty tang of the ham, the sharpness of the cheese, and the richness of the white sauce were pure perfection. I always loved waffles, but this was waffles on a whole other level.

"One last breakfast together," she said, chin on her hands as she sat across from me and watched me eat. "I'll be seeing you when I can, but probably not for breakfast. Not for quite some time."

"Brunch works for me," I said between bites. "Or tea time."

She just smiled.

Although my back was to the eastern window, I could sense the sky there lightening by the minute. The sun would be up soon. I finished off my waffle and the last of my coffee, then went to get into my parka, hat, and mittens.

I handed my grandmother the duffel that held my clothes since it was the lighter of the two bags, then hoisted my art bags onto my own back. I had both my usual one that I carried with me everywhere with my sketching implements in it and a larger one that held all of my other tools. Bottles of ink clacked together as I hefted it up into place.

Then I picked up my easel, collapsed into its most portable form, and looped an arm through the carrying strap so that it rested on my back on top of my other two bags.

It was a lot to carry. Luckily, we didn't have far to go.

Unluckily, the bit we did have to go was mostly uphill, on a narrow rocky trail that was always slick and wet from the waterfall that cascaded just a few feet away.

The sky overhead was immense and cloudless, but the sun about to rise behind us was winking out the stars one by one. No wind stirred the air, but it was so cold it hurt to breathe, and I kept the collar of my parka zipped up over my nose.

No birds were out and the lack of wind made the lake itself unusually silent, but the rush of water in the river beside the path was joined by the faint hum of the occasional early morning truck crossing the bridge across the gorge far over our heads. But soon even that engine sound was drowned out by the roar of the waterfall.

We climbed without speaking, although I could hear my grandmother's breath even through the layers of scarf she had wrapped around the bottom of her face. At last we reached the turn in the path from steeply climbing uphill to narrowly ducking behind the cascading water.

Usually the cave behind the waterfall felt like a relief to reach, a shelter from the elements. It was a place to pause and unzip coats and pull off woolen hats and mittens before pressing on to the deeper chambers. But since the morning was windless, the air behind the waterfall was no warmer than out on the rocky bluff, and the droplets that always sprayed across the cavern were quite icy.

My grandmother pulled the scarf down off her nose only long enough to call out, "Which Thor is guarding?"

I was hoping to hear Thorbjorn's voice, but it was his younger brother who answered. "Well met, Nora Torfudottir. It is I, Thorge, who guards."

Then we heard the sound of stone grinding on stone, and the light from the distant bonfire flickered down the turn of the cave that suddenly appeared before us.

We hustled in to reach the warmth of the bonfire. I could smell its familiar smell, some type of wood I couldn't identify but was always the same. Like how my grandmother's kitchen always smelled like coffee and waffles, this place had a smell of its own that felt like a different kind of home to me.

Thorge was waiting for us at the stone doorway, and after we passed through, he rolled it closed again behind us. I wasn't sure if this was about the cold or some new security measure, or if Thorge was just more cautious when he was on guard than some of his brothers.

I gave him a questioning glance, but he just gave me a warm smile of welcome. "Well met, Ingrid Torfudottir," he said.

"Well met, Thorge Valkisson," I said. His words to me had flowed naturally off his tongue, so why did my response sound so stilting and formal?

We had only met once before, on the night that he and his brothers had fought the trolls that were aiding in a Villmarker's flight from justice. I glanced up at the elaborate knot work tattoos that arced over his ears. His long red hair was shaved on the sides to show them off, and I still longed to sketch them into one of my books, to really study the pattern. I didn't think they were actual magic, but they had some meaning, surely.

But now was probably not the time. With a sigh, I followed my grandmother to stand by the bonfire.

"Is there some kind of ritual?" I asked as I held my mittened hands out to the warmth of the fire.

"No," my grandmother said, bemused, as if I had asked the oddest sort of question.

"I was supposed to be here by sunrise," I said. "I thought there would be some sort of... reception?"

"No, nothing like that," my grandmother said. She too had been warming her hands at the fire, but now she clapped her hands together as if declaring herself warm enough to continue. "Shall we?"

"I suppose," I said. Thorge waved farewell to us, then settled onto one of the three-legged stools by the bonfire to continue his watch. "So the sunrise thing was just a deadline?" I asked my grandmother as we walked up the natural stone steps at the back of the cave and up to the meadow that overlooked the waterfall, the town of Runde, and the lake beyond.

"Not everything is magic," she told me. "That doesn't make it less important to be on time."

"No, I suppose not," I agreed. But it was disconcerting to yet again have to adjust my expectations. I wouldn't have to keep adjusting if people would just be straight with me about what was going on.

We walked through the little forest to the village of Villmark. The streets were empty and silent, but there were lights on in some of the windows as people within began to stir. We continued straight on to the well that stood in the center of the square that was once the village commons.

When the original settlers had built the first iteration of the village, they had built their homes around this central square to keep the few cows and goats they had brought with them safe from wolves. As the village had grown, the dairy herds had moved to the valley south of the village and the village itself had taken on more of a grid of roads type of layout. The commons, no longer needed for grazing animals, had shrunk to a mere square at the crossroads.

The only thing that had persisted through all that time was the well which still stood at the center.

Not that anyone used it for water anymore. Every house had indoor plumbing now. But the only thing in Villmark that was older than the well was the bonfire in the cave behind the waterfall.

My grandmother and I turned left at the square. The house she had grown up in, our ancestral home, was only a few doors down on the right from that well. She led the way up the walk and inside the house, setting my duffel of clothes and her walking stick just inside the door and pulling off her boots before heading further inside to turn on light after light.

I left my easel and art bags by my duffel of clothes but took off my parka, hat and mittens as well as my boots before stepping up out of the entranceway into the main part of the house.

My house. My grandmother had made that clear on many occasions. She had grown up here, but it was no longer home to her now. Her heart's home was her cabin in Runde, and especially the mead hall she kept that stood where Runde and Villmark overlapped. This place was mine now.

Only it didn't feel like it.

I rubbed at my arms as I passed the cozy little kitchen tucked off the corridor, close to the front door, and stepped into the great room.

The north and east sides of the house were divided into two stories, but the south and west half was all one room, this room. The north end rose up half a level, almost like a dais, which effectively set off about a third of the floor space closest to the stairs to the second level.

The rising sun was not yet visible through the south-facing floor to ceiling windows, but its light was shining on the frost-covered trees of the hills.

"Everything is in order," my grandmother said, and I looked up to see her coming out of one of the bedrooms on the second floor. "I had some things removed, but just little personal things. Every room is furnished, and you can take whichever one you like. Move the furniture where you want it, add or remove anything, don't feel like you have to ask permission from me."

"Okay," I said. My voice sounded small, like that big empty room was just swallowing it up.

"Well, your friends have already been here adding things, I see," she said. At first I didn't know what she meant, but when she came into the great room to stand beside me, I followed her gaze to take in a stack of wrapped packages left on the row of built-in benches along the eastern wall.

"My friends?" I said as I crossed the room to look closely at the brown wrapping. There was no card, and nothing was written on the paper.

"Loke dropped those off, unless I'm very much mistaken," my grandmother said. "Coffee?"

Normally I didn't drink even as much coffee as I had had before we'd left her house less than an hour ago. But I hadn't slept, and I knew it was going to be a long day. "Do I have any?" I asked.

"I brought some," she said, then disappeared into the kitchen.

I turned my attention to the packages. They were flat and rectangular, but it was definitely not boxes inside, as nothing rattled when I shook them. I carefully unwrapped the paper.

What I saw under the paper brought a well of emotion to my throat. They were my own pen and ink drawings of different places around Runde. My grandmother's cabin, the banks of the river, tree-lined views of the lake. Not mere sketches but finished drawings I had done, then tossed onto the pile of things I might someday put up for sale on Jessica's café wall.

But someone had taken them and framed them. I ran my fingertips over the wood of the frames. Real wood, cut and finished by hand.

Somehow, I just knew they were Andrew's work. It was like I could feel him there with me when I touched those frames. Like I could smell him standing just behind me.

Which was silly. I could smell the frames, new as they were, but not specifically him. It was just a strong association. Andrew always smelled of wood and stain, and usually had bits of each clinging to the wool of his sweaters.

And just as surely as I knew the frames were from Andrew, I knew that it was Loke who had brought these here. It was Loke who knew just what I needed to make this foreign-feeling place feel a little more like my home.

My grandmother came back in and handed me one of the mugs of coffee she was carrying and I set the pictures aside to take it.

"That's lovely," she said as she picked one up to look at it more closely. "Yes, I told him this was a good idea."

"Loke," I guessed.

"Hmm," she agreed as she sipped at her coffee. "Of course Andrew was involved as well. He picked out which drawings to pilfer from you, but I was sure you wouldn't mind."

"Not in the least," I said.

"I'm sure they'll look lovely wherever you decide to hang them," she said, looking around. Nothing changed on her face, and her tone was still cheery, but her next words were a bit chilling. "You know, I never quite liked this house."

"Really?" I said. I thought the coldness was something only I felt, because this was all still new to me. But she had grown up in this house.

"Oh, nothing tragic," she assured me. "I had a perfectly lovely childhood, and two parents who adored me. It just never felt like I belonged here. Well, lots of kids feel that way, don't they? And then..."

But she trailed off, giving herself a little shake and then me a reassuring smile.

"Never mind, dear," she said. "A story for another time."

She was still smiling, but I knew that no matter how I begged, she wasn't going to finish what she had been about to say until she was good and ready.

And as it turned out, she wouldn't have had time to anyway, as at that very minute there was a knock at the door.

"That will be Nilda and Kara," my grandmother said as she waved me towards the door. "They promised to stock your pantry and will likely have gifts as well."

I could tell my grandmother was right before I even opened the door. The smell of fresh-baked bread preceded my two friends, and my mouth was watering despite my belly still being full of waffles.

Then I swung the door open, and that smell wafted past me. It was almost like I could see it moving down the hall, spreading throughout the house, mingling with the smell of my grandmother's coffee to dispel the older, staler smells of a too-long-empty house.

We hadn't even built up a fire yet, but my friends were already warming my house for me.

CHAPTER THREE

THE FOUR OF us unpacked all the boxes Nilda and Kara had brought with them, putting a bunch of pantry staples into cupboards that already contained plates and cups, cookware and bakeware that looked old-fashioned but little-used. They had gotten some fresh items as well, milk and butter and a couple of apples, which went into the little refrigerator in the corner. It was about the size of a dorm fridge meant for beverages and takeout leftovers, but its sturdy design struck me as more like an old-school icebox.

And it plugged into the wall. Which shouldn't be surprising, since I had seen electric lights all over Villmark. But it was one more thing I had taken for granted that I now realized I didn't know: where their electricity came from.

But Nilda and Kara were chatting happily with my grandmother, joking and laughing as they worked. I didn't want to break the mood with a bunch of technical questions. I would be here all the time now. There would be more than enough opportunities to get all those answers in the days ahead.

Then, after the last of the food was put away, my grandmother turned to me. "It's time for me to go."

"Already?" I asked. My voice didn't quite squeak, but it was close.

"I have things to do before this evening," she said, and I more than knew that was true. She would be doing the magic alone again, without me there to help her. "Your friends will take care of you from here," she said.

"We have more boxes in the garden still to bring in yet," Nilda told me. "Decorative elements and such."

"Of course we'll want to see what needs to be moved around in here first," Kara said, looking up towards the stairs to the top floor where the bedrooms were. "We'll have this place rearranged to fit your style in no time."

I fought a yawn. Neither Kara nor Nilda saw it, but I could tell by the gleam in my grandmother's eye as she pressed a quick kiss to my cheek that she had.

I had been expecting that she would leave before lunchtime. The magic she did to turn the Runde meeting hall into the mead hall was a complex interweaving of dozens of separate spells. It had to be to allow the inhabitants of Villmark and Runde to intermix without the residents of Runde ever remembering that they spent their evenings among the living descendants of the Viking Age.

They had to forget, to keep the people of Villmark safe. But it was exhausting magic for any volva, let alone my grandmother, who I knew was older than she looked, even if I didn't know exactly how old that was.

And I would no longer be able to help her, not even the little bit I had been managing over the last few weeks. I felt a twinge of guilt about that, but reminded myself that the entire reason I was in Villmark was to grow and strengthen my magical powers. When I returned, I would be more help to her. I might even be able to give her a night or two off.

I stood in my stocking feet on my front step and watched until my grandmother reached the square. She turned back and gave me a little wave.

And then she was gone.

I went back inside and shut the door, but before I could quite feel sad or lonely, my friends came rushing to take my hands and lead me back into the house.

The two of them had already decided we should start with the bedroom that was going to be mine now. We climbed the stairs to the second floor, then followed the corridor past the two smaller north-facing bedrooms to the larger bedroom over the kitchen.

It was enormous, more room than two people needed, and it was all for me now. The bed was set against the western wall, since the east and south sides were nothing but windows. The sun was tracking its way westward, but this close to the solstice it was clearly never going to rise higher than the top of the window. The room was filled with cheery sunshine, made all the brighter by the ice and snow covering everything in view outside.

"This is amazing," Kara said, but she wasn't talking about the view. She was running her hands over the top of the massive dresser, then brushing her fingertips over the front of a tall wooden wardrobe. She opened the doors, but the inside was empty. So were the drawers of the dresser.

"This might not be so much work after all," Nilda said.

"No, mormor said she already took away everything she wanted to keep, and I think she got rid of a lot of other things as well," I said. "She's been up here in Villmark more in the last three days than she ever has since I've been here."

"And we like the bedding?" Nilda asked, pointing with both hands toward the bed that was bigger than a king-size. I ran my hand over the duvet. It was thicker than it looked, the comforter within heavy and surely warm. And the icy blue color was a lovely reflection of the sky outside, nicely contrasted by a mound of snowy white and dark blue pillows.

"I do," I said.

"Then we'll just toss your duffle in here and you can unpack your clothes later," Nilda said.

"But wait!" Kara said, catching her arm. "There was that other thing."

"Oh, right," Nilda said conspiratorially.

"What are we talking about?" I asked.

Kara grinned at me. "We got you a little something. Well, two little somethings, but they go together."

My confusion must have shown on my face, because Nilda said to her sister, "we should just show her."

Kara nodded, still grinning, then ran down the stairs. I heard the door slam once as she went out, then again when she came back in a moment later.

Then she was back in the room, a pillow-like something in her hands. She looked around, then seemed to find just the spot she was looking for. She set the thing on the floor between the side of the bed and the small fireplace that separated that sleeping space from where the wardrobe and dresser defined what I was already thinking of as the dressing area.

"It's for Mjolner," Kara said.

"A cat bed," I said. I hated to break it to her, but Mjolner would surely spurn it in favor of dominating whatever pillow I was using. But it did look cozy there, just on the edge of the rug that looked like a white bearskin spread across the wood floor before the fireplace.

Surely it wasn't a bearskin. The only polar bears in Minnesota were safely protected inside of zoos.

Of course there was the wilds north of town, where the hills of Minnesota faded into the mountains of old Norway, with a side trip into Iceland. And that was just what I knew of that place from one short, if all too thrilling, trip. I wouldn't be surprised if polar bears were to be found somewhere further in than I had gone. I mean, I had seen trolls, and that felt a lot more inconceivable than polar bears.

We continued on to the other two rooms, smaller but no less lavishly furnished. These beds had drawers beneath them, empty now, and similarly thick duvets, one cream-colored and the other a forest green.

If there had been any way to know which room had been my grandmother's when she had been a girl, there was no clue now. I thought it might be the second one with the green duvet, the one closest to the top of the stairs. It just had a kind of energy to it that made me feel safe and protected.

Then I looked out its north-facing window and could just make out the furthest house on the northern road, the home of the Thors. Maybe that was where this safe feeling was coming from.

The rest of the day passed in a blur of activity. We spent the bulk of our time downstairs in the great room. I let Nilda and Kara decide where to hang my drawings, what rug should go next to the larger downstairs fireplace, which pillows and throws should liven up the long benches along the walls.

I had never cared much for decorating myself. Besides, while they did all that, I was busy doing what felt like the most important part of moving in: setting up my easel and other art supplies.

I picked the western-most end of the room just under the little dais, a spot sufficiently out of the way of the main room for my artwork not to be disturbed by guests. It was close enough so that I could still see out the windows, but far enough that there wasn't going to be the full glare of that sun in my eyes when I was working.

I dragged over a tall but narrow bookcase that had been standing empty at the other end of the room. Then I fetched a three-legged stool that had been sitting by the fireplace. Then I set up my easel, settled down on that stool, and started deciding where each of my tools should go so they would be neatly arranged on that bookcase but in easy reach from the stool.

I changed my mind a lot, rearranging what I had already unpacked almost every time I unpacked something new. There wasn't even any paper on the easel in front of me, but still I found myself sinking into a flow state, where my mind was on nothing but art. I was just lost in the idea of all I would create here, in my new space.

I don't know how long I was absorbed like that, but I got the sense that Nilda and Kara had called my name several times before I finally looked up.

"Sorry," I said. "What is it?"

"Mjolner is here," Kara said. "I think he likes his bed."

I leaned around the easel to see my polydactyl black cat sprawled out on a pillow that was a twin to the one Kara had put upstairs. He stretched out, licked the tip of his own nose, then sank into a deep cat-sleep.

"I guess he feels at home here, anyway," I said.

"You don't?" Kara asked, sounding disappointed.

"Well, I don't know yet," I said. "It looks great, though. Very cozy."

"You like it?" she asked, looking around like she wasn't sure.

"We can get rid of anything that doesn't suit you," Nilda said. "You won't hurt our feelings."

"We went a little nuts," Kara said. "We talk about getting our own place together, but somehow we just keep living with our folks."

"Our mother would never let us rearrange her stuff like this," Nilda said, toying with a pillow on one of the benches.

"No, it really does look great," I said. "I'm sure in a few days I'll feel right at home here."

"Oh, of course," Kara agreed. "A few nights sleeping in that bed upstairs, and you'll just settle right in here."

I wanted to agree but was interrupted by a massive yawn.

"Sorry," I said. "I think I need a nap."

"No, you don't want to do that now," Nilda said. "It's just going to mess up your sleep tonight if you nap this late."

"This late?" I repeated, then belatedly noticed that the sun had sunk low over the hills to the west. Of course it went down early this time of year, but still. I had lost track of hours and hours.

"We should get something to eat," Kara said.

"My kitchen is fully stocked," I said.

"I meant we should go out," Kara said, coming around the easel to catch hold of my arm and pull me to my feet. "Your main job here is to integrate with the community, right? You have to go out and be with others to accomplish that."

"Just dinner," Nilda said in a voice that made it clear she was the older sister. "We won't make it a late night."

"Not tonight," Kara said, but the way she said it sounded almost like a threat. Like there were a bunch of late nights coming for me, just over the horizon.

CHAPTER FOUR

WE BUNDLED up and headed out into the cold, quickly darkening evening. The streetlights were coming on one by one, their light shuttered to shine down on the road and not up into the sky. I had never seen an airplane pass overhead, but surely something must at some point. Satellites up in space, for instance. I wondered what Villmark looked like from up there. Or did the spells hide it, even from satellite cameras?

"This way," Nilda said, pulling me out of my thoughts with a tug on the sleeve of my parka. I followed her and Kara along the road away from the center of town, south to the public gardens. We followed a path through canvas-wrapped and snow-covered hedges, across the gardens and past the greenhouses to an A-framed building that stood alone on the far side.

It looked old, the wooden support beams carved into the shapes of fantastical animals. I thought it might be a sod roof under all that snow, but there was no way to be sure. The double doors stood open, and warm firelight from within lit up the cobblestone street in front of it.

I had only been to one mead hall in Villmark, and that had been a similarly old-styled building, but as soon as we were inside I knew the comparisons stopped there. That place had been dark and closed-in, filled with dangerous types who had been keeping to themselves but with an air of menace, as if it would be easy to disturb them out of that aloofness and into something a lot more combative.

The mood of this place was very different. Beyond those invitingly opened doors was a short flight of stairs, the floor of the hall set nearly five feet below ground level. This made the sod roof above soar overhead, creating a large and open space below. The tables were arranged more like in my grandmother's mead hall down in Runde, in long rows that invited different groups to sit together. To eat, drink and make merry together.

But it was early yet, and we looked at first to be the only customers.

Then I saw Loke sitting at one of those tables with a mug of beer before him. He saw us come in and raised a hand in greeting.

"Loke!" I said, skirting an open fire pit covered with hot grates ready and waiting to start roasting meat to reach his side. "Thank you for the lovely housewarming gift."

He waved a dismissive hand as he took a sip of his beer. "Don't mention it. It was Andrew's idea, anyway. I was just the delivery boy."

"I thought Thorbjorn was going to be here," Kara said, looking around as if a redhead the size of a linebacker might be hiding somewhere behind one of the narrow wooden beams.

"I'll get us some food," Nilda said, taking off her coat and hanging it from a hook on one of those beams before turning to me. "You have to have the meatballs first. I'm not even kidding. You've never had meatballs like Ullr's special meatballs."

"Of course," I said. I watched her disappear through a door at the back of the hall before leaning closer to Loke to whisper. "It's just like Swedish meatballs, right?"

Loke gave me a look of mock offense. "Don't let Ullr hear you say that. You'll be banned for life for a comment like that one."

"Seriously?" I asked.

"You really want to be testing the boundaries already?" he asked. "Maybe try blending in a little first."

"Loke, have *you* seen Thorbjorn?" Kara asked as she finally stopped searching the empty hall and slid onto the bench across from us.

"On occasion," Loke said drily. "But not lately. I believe he is on patrol."

"Oh," Kara said. She looked dejected for a moment, but brightened when Nilda came back to the table with a plate of meatballs in each hand. A tiny young woman I assumed was a server came behind her with another pair of plates.

Ullr's meatballs weren't remotely like Swedish meatballs. I had always loved Swedish meatballs, but this was something else entirely. I couldn't name all the spices that were mixed in with the meat, and the brown sauce was buttery but not creamy. And the mashed root vegetable they were resting on was rutabaga, not potato.

By the time I was mopping up the last of the sauce with some of the brown bread that had magically appeared on the table in the center of our little group, other people had started gathering at either end of the table around us. The other table was filling up as well, and the room was warm with the heat of so many bodies. Kara kept looking up constantly, and I knew she was still watching for Thorbjorn.

I wasn't sure how I felt about that. I had known she thought he was good-looking, but anyone who saw him would have to think that. It was just empirically true.

But clearly her interest was deeper than I had thought. And for some reason, it felt like something was clenching at my heart.

But it couldn't be jealousy, could it? Because Thorbjorn and I were just friends.

Weren't we?

I glanced over at Loke, half expecting him to be watching my face and reading my thoughts with a teasing comment at the ready.

But he wasn't looking at me. His gaze was directed across the room. Then he got up without a word, pushing through the crowd as he headed towards the doorway before returning with a companion in tow.

Roarr.

"Hey, all," Roarr said, his face flushed as if embarrassed by something. "Can I sit with you?"

"The more the merrier," Nilda said, and I moved over so he could squeeze in between me and where Loke was resuming his place.

"I had to rescue him from the clutches of far too many predators," Loke said as he turned his attention back to his meatballs.

"I wasn't in need of rescue," Roarr said, but the way his cheeks further reddened made me think that wasn't entirely true.

"Still getting swarmed by suitors?" I asked. As if in answer to my question, that little serving woman appeared out of nowhere to put an overloaded plate of meatballs before Roarr. He just barely glanced at her and mumbled a quick thanks before digging in.

"Excuse me," Kara said suddenly and hopped up off the bench to run to someone just coming in the door.

Nilda sighed and shook her head, but there was an indulgent smile on her face.

"This is new?" I asked.

"What, Kara? Yeah," Nilda said. Loke and Roarr were speaking together in low voices directly across from her, so she slid into her sister's spot and leaned across the table towards me.

"How are you doing?" she asked as she took my hands in hers. "Homesick yet?"

"No," I said. But it suddenly struck me what an odd thought that was, being homesick. I had only lived in Runde for a few months. Before that, I had spent my entire life in St. Paul. I had spent nearly every night of my life in the same bed, in the same bedroom, in the same house, until one day I just didn't anymore.

And I had never missed it. I hadn't even realized I hadn't missed it until just this very moment. I had never been homesick for St. Paul. And I didn't feel homesick for Runde now.

But maybe that was because I had never felt at home before? I had always used my art to escape to other places, other worlds entirely, ever since I was old enough to clutch a crayon and make marks on paper. Was that because I had been searching for a home all this time?

Was Villmark that home?

It was my turn to heave a sigh. "I don't know?" I finally said.

"Sleepover at your house, then?" Nilda asked. "I'm sure Kara will be up for it."

"No, I'll be okay," I said. "It's time for me to be alone in that house, I think."

"Of course," Nilda said, and gave my hands a squeeze. "But you know where I live if you ever need me."

"I do," I agreed. Then I saw Kara returning. Nilda turned to follow my line of sight, then got to her feet as her sister came back to the bench with a pair of blonde twins in tow. Sigvin and her sister Nefja. I had met them separately before but was seeing them standing side by side for the first time.

They gave me the same welcoming smile as I reached across the table to shake their hands. But then one of them stopped smiling, her face falling despondently. I tried to remember which was which. I knew that one of them had their little freckle on the left and the other had it on the right, but I couldn't remember which sister went with which freckle.

Then I realized Loke had just disappeared, leaving without a farewell, and I unlocked the mystery.

If Loke had just fled, the only person I'd ever met who could be so sad to see him go - and, in fact, the only person I had ever seen him flee from - was Sigvin.

So the crestfallen one with the freckle on her right cheek was Sigvin. Which made the sister with the freckle on her left cheek, the one desperately trying to catch Roarr's eye, Nefja.

Poor Roarr. He seemed frozen on that bench, trying not to meet Nefja's eyes while simultaneously sneaking looks around, trying to figure out where Loke had gone.

I sat back down beside him and leaned over to whisper in his ear, "don't worry. I'll keep you safe."

He gave me a puzzled look, like he hadn't understood my words. Then the serving woman was back, leaning between us to refill his mug with ale. By the time she had finished and had disappeared again, Roarr seemed to have worked out what I had meant. He gave me a grateful smile, then reached for another plate of meatballs that had magically appeared on the table in front of him.

He might balk at all the attention he got as a single man in Vill-mark, but clearly it had an upside. And if he truly had no interest in any of these women, they would soon have him fattened him up enough to be a less hot item on the dating market.

Somehow, I didn't think that concept would bother him at all.

CHAPTER FIVE

I STAYED up later than I had intended to, eating and talking with Nilda, Kara, Sigvin and Nefja. Any worry I had that I might have trouble getting to sleep in my house was gone long before I stumbled inside in the wee hours of the morning and collapsed onto the bed, completely exhausted.

I was vaguely aware of Mjolner hopping onto the bed and making himself comfortable on my pillow. He curled up against the back of my neck and immediately started loudly purring, but by about the third purr sleep took me and I knew no more.

I woke a handful of hours later when the first rays of the rising sun beaming in through my many windows reached the head of my bed.

I would have to decide at some point if I was going to be a morning person now, or if curtains were in order. But not yet. The only thing on my mind at that moment was coffee and the need to go downstairs to make it.

Once I was dressed and had a cup of coffee in me, I finally turned my attention to the day before me.

I was supposed to start my lessons with Haraldr today, only I didn't know when or where. I opened my front door and looked for any sort of message, then crossed the front garden to check the gate, but there was nothing.

I went back inside, uncertain what to do. I knew some Villmarkers had cellphones, but I doubted Haraldr was one of them, and even if he were, I had no idea what his number was. And it was barely past dawn, way too early to wake anyone else up to ask for help.

I wandered over to my art corner and looked at my carefully arranged supplies. I had half a thought to just start sketching something to kill the time until it was a reasonable hour for other people to be up when Mjolner came down the stairs. He stopped at the bottom, stretched with an enormous cat yawn, and shook himself from the whiskers around his nose to the tip of his tail, then gave me a look.

I knew that look. He wanted me to follow him.

I stopped at the door to bundle up in parka and boots, hat and mittens, but Mjolner went on ahead without me in that way he did where he apparently just walked through walls. I had never seen him do it, but there was no other explanation for how no door was ever an obstacle to him.

Outside it was another sunny but cold day, the light reflecting off the snow almost blinding. Mjolner was pacing outside my garden gate, but the moment I stepped out into the street he immediately turned to the south, towards the public gardens. Despite my mittens, my hands were still cold, and I thrust them deep inside my pockets before I followed.

The house he led me to was much like the others, of a minimalist but modern Scandinavian design that favored clean, straight lines and lots of south-facing windows. I had half-expected a cottage like the witch Halldis had lived in just a couple of blocks away, with its round Hobbit door and peaked roof.

Mjolner hopped up onto one of the fence posts across the street from this house and started licking his paw and grooming himself, completely heedless of the cold that was making my cheeks burn.

I hustled up the walk and knocked on the door, the sound a bit muffled by my mitten.

I hoped I had the right place. It was still on the early side to be waking strangers or interrupting their breakfast.

The door was opened by a girl of maybe thirteen with dark blonde hair in two braids that hung over her shoulders. My heart sank. Haraldr was too old for this to be his daughter; I had gotten the wrong house. I shot a glare back over my shoulder at Mjolner, who ignored me, then turned back to apologize to the girl.

"You're Ingrid Torfudottir?" she asked me in careful English before I could get a word out. She was peering up at my hat as if hoping for a glimpse of my distinctive red hair to answer her question.

"I am," I said. "Is this Haraldr's house?"

"It is," she said. "I'm Fulla. I'm Haraldr's... assistant?" She gave me a questioning look, and I nodded that she had the right word. "I help in his house and in his library. He's expecting you. Will you come in?"

"Thank you," I said, stomping the snow off my boots before stepping inside. She shut the door behind me, then helped me hang up my parka. She took my hat and mittens and stuffed them down my parka's sleeve as I undid my bootlaces and stepped out of my boots. Then she led me down a long corridor to the heart of the house.

There were a series of doorways on my right leading into first a little sitting room, then a dining room, then a kitchen. But Fulla continued on to the only door on the left, knocking briefly but not waiting for a response before turning the handle and opening the door.

"Haraldr, Ingrid is here," she said. I couldn't see whom she was speaking to. All I could see were books. Shelves and shelves of books. The room ran the length of the house and was two stories tall with a little balcony running all around halfway up those towering shelves. The morning sun was shining in through low horizontal windows set across the tops of the cases.

"Oh, dear," Fulla said, turning to Ingrid with a frown. "I thought he was in here already. Can you wait here? I'll go find him."

"Certainly," I said with a smile. Then she went back out the door, closing it carefully behind her, and I was alone with all those books.

It seemed wisest not to touch anything, so I folded my hands together behind my back as I made a slow circuit of the room. Some books were new, hardcovers from New York publishers on a variety of topics. Others were old, bound in leather that was cracked and faded with time. There were also racks of scrolls and even stacks of wooden staves that had been carved with runes like the unbound pages of a wooden book.

There was also art. Little carvings were arranged in glass cases that appeared to be locked. I recognized Norse artifacts, arrowheads and sewing needles and other bits of daily life from centuries past. But others looked to my eye like Ojibwe work.

A massive desk stood at the southern-most end of the room. There was a large window here, but it was set high above the level of the balcony that stretched across it like a catwalk. On the wall directly in front of me, behind that desk's chair, was a massive drawing of the World Tree.

It had been painted directly on the wall, and the closer I stepped to it, the more intricate I realized it was. I scanned image after image worked among the branches of Yggdrasil. Gods fighting giants, Norns gathered around a well, a dragon talking with a squirrel. Was every Norse legend I knew somewhere in this drawing? I suspected it was, but it would take hours and hours to be sure.

"Ah, Ingrid," Haraldr said, standing directly behind me. I hadn't heard the door open or his footsteps as he approached, and I jumped guiltily at the sound of his voice. "It *is* a work of art, isn't it?"

"Did you do it?" I asked.

"No, that was my grandfather's hand," he said. "Come, let's sit together at the other end of the room." He waved for me to follow him. I gave the mural one last longing glance, then turned to follow Haraldr to the north end of the room.

There was no window here, just one massive stone fireplace, the hearth spanning nearly the entire width of the room. The bookcases ended a respectable distance away, as if roaring fires were common-place on that hearth. There was nothing burning there now, but still Haraldr pulled up a three-legged stool and motioned for me to sit there, then pulled another over for himself.

"Now," he said, rubbing his hands over his knees and looking around as if for inspiration.

"What spells are we going to start with?" I asked eagerly.

"No spells, not yet," he said. Then he seemed to remember something and hopped up from the stool, shuffling over to a little cabinet built into one of the bookcases and digging around inside.

When he returned to his stool, I saw that he had a little leather bag in his hand. He loosened the bindings, then stirred a finger around inside. I could hear wooden pieces rattling against each other, and when he pulled out a single tile and showed it to me, I was scarcely surprised to see it was a rune.

"Tell me what you know of this particular rune," he said, holding it out towards me on his open palm. I made no move to take it from him. I didn't know for sure if that would be taboo, but I knew how some people felt about other people touching their Tarot decks and decided to err on the side of caution.

"That's called Fe," I said, glancing up at his face to see if I had that right. His face told me nothing, and I looked back down at the rune. It looked like a letter F, but rather than two horizontal strokes there were two that angled up at about forty-five degrees. "It makes a 'fff' sound?" I added, even less sure about that than I had been about the first thing.

I expected him to sigh, to show some exasperation, but he didn't. He just retracted his hand and looked at the rune tile as if double-checking before he spoke. "You are correct, so far as you go," Haraldr said. "Do you know anything about its meaning?"

"Not really," I admitted. "I've only ever used the runes to spell out words in my illustrations. I know it's the first rune in the futhark, though. Hence the 'f' in futhark."

"Very good," he said as he put the tile back in his leather bag. "So tell me, what came first in the creation of the world?"

I nearly said, "the Big Bang," but bit my tongue just in time. "Fire and ice?" I said instead.

"The uplift of your voice at the end of that sentence tells me you know that's not quite right," he said. "Think. You know the stories."

I remembered something about a giant's skull, but I was sure that had come a lot later than the fire and the ice. But wasn't ice the oldest thing of all?

Then I remembered. "The cow."

"Audhumbla," he agreed, nodding.

"She's licking the ice, and she licks out the first three gods. Odin and his brothers."

"See, you knew more than you thought," he said.

"Well, I'm pretty sure it's barely scratching the surface," I said.

"It's a start," he said almost sternly. "That's your learning's start. Know now there is no end to your learning. Not with the runes, not with anything worth knowing. Seeking true knowledge is walking a road with no end."

"Okay," I said. I was a little worried I had made him angry, but then the sternness melted away and he started turning the rune tile around and around on his hand.

"The runes are three sets of eight. You know this?" he asked. I shook my head. "Yes, this is so. The first set of eight belongs to the god Frey. They are runes of creation, of the origin of certain things, but even of all things. All life comes from these runes, and everything that happens has its beginnings here."

I nodded, wishing I had brought a notebook.

"So Fe is the first cow, what does that suggest to you?" he asked.

"Milk?" I guessed. "Wait, didn't her milk make the Milky Way?"

"Yes, but forget Audhumbla for a moment. What does an ordinary cow represent to a family?"

My hands twitched. I was so much better at answering these sorts of questions if I could just let my mind go and draw, then look at my drawing later. But if I drew a family with their cow, or cows maybe, what would that mean?

"Wealth?" I said, very tentatively. "Milk and butter and cheese from one cow can keep a family alive. From a lot of cows, a family could make more than a living."

"And what can you do with money?" he asked.

"Spend it," I said. He just looked at me, and I realized he wanted me to say more. "Save it, I guess. Or invest it."

"And how do you get money in the first place?"

I was starting to warm up to this. "Earn it, like with a job, or inherit it. Like land."

"Or like cattle," he agreed, nodding. "The proper nature of money is to be always in motion. Earned or spent, saved or invested, but always moving through society. Through my hands or through yours. It's like energy, always on the move."

"Okay," I said. "So cows are money."

"Not just money," he said with a little wave of his hand. "Money is only part of it. There is another thing that's more important. Do you know the word hamingja?"

I had heard it, but I had never quite understood it. "Like karma?" I said lamely.

"Similar," he said. "But karma concerns just one soul. It extends across one's previous life and current one and future ones, but still it's just one soul. Hamingja is similar, but it's like a soul that belongs to an entire family line."

"Like how my grandmother is a volva and I will be too one day?" I asked.

He made a little tipping motion of his head, and I knew he only partially agreed with that assessment. "It's not the same as a calling, although sometimes that's part of it. It's more like luck, a luck you inherit based on the good and noble deeds of your ancestors. You inherit some amount, and you can either increase it throughout your life through good and noble deeds, or diminish it through weak or dishonorable ones. Then, when you die, whatever amount you possessed passes on to your descendants."

"I guess like money," I said. "If I inherit a fortune and squander it, there's nothing left for my offspring."

"Or if you inherit nothing but amass a fortune, that is where they will start," Haraldr said.

"I'm not sure I like that idea," I said after thinking it over for a moment.

"Why not?" he asked, completely unoffended.

"Well, it doesn't seem fair," I said. "I mean, life's not fair, sure, but that seems *particularly* unfair. Some people are born luckier than others? I mean, weren't they already lucky just to be born to lucky parents?"

"Ah, you're already getting it," he said with a wide smile. "Everything in life is easier when luck is on your side."

"But still," I said. "It feels like it should be spread around more equally." Although how I thought that was going to happen, I had no idea.

It wasn't like I quite believed these gods were real. I knew the magic was, and I knew trolls were real, but Odin and Thor and the rest? It was a pretty big leap for my mind to make.

"If you don't like what you started life out with, it's within your power to change it," Haraldr said. "And when you do change it, you make life better for those that follow you. Of course you don't really have to worry. Your family line is one of the strongest we know. Perhaps *the* strongest."

I squirmed on my stool. Somehow, knowing the world was unfair, but I was benefiting from it just made me feel worse about everything.

"Isn't there anything we can do about the people who are born unlucky?" I asked.

"They must do it themselves or it means nothing," Haraldr said. "A person born into such a family will have to understand how their low hamingja influences how others see them, certainly. But there is no reason for them to feel trapped by those circumstances. Our gods more than most love an underdog."

"I suppose," I said. It seemed best not to speak my earlier thought out loud, about not really believing in these gods as real. Although I was pretty sure Haraldr guessed it from how he was looking at me just then.

"Here," he said, getting up from his stool and going back to that cabinet. He put the leather pouch away, then scrounged around again until he had a stiff square of plain cardboard in his hand. He then went to the cold fireplace and jabbed a finger into the ash pile. Then he scrawled the Fe shape onto the card with that sooty fingertip before handing it to me. "Take this home. Meditate on it. See what you discover."

"I will," I promised, looking at the dark, gritty shape on the card. If I put it in my pocket, it would surely smear. I kept it in my hand.

"Oh, one word of warning," he said as he opened the door back out to the hallway. "This will be true with all the runes, so mark me well. We'll progress through them one at a time, and as we go, you'll learn how to bond with them more quickly and surely. But when you first start meditating on them, it's not unusual to start seeing their shape everywhere in the world around you. This is a very positive rune, so you might not find that alarming, but keep it in mind for when we get to some of the others. This will just be your mind being too focused on one rune at the expense of all the others. It's not a true omen of any sort."

"I'll remember," I promised.

"I'm sure you will," he said, nodding as he spoke, but it felt like he was agreeing with himself. Like I was already out of his mind.

"When should I call again?" I asked.

"Hmm?" he looked up at me as if surprised to see me still standing there. I was about to repeat my question when he spoke again. "Oh, tomorrow morning will be fine. Meditate on that rune. And I'm sure you'll dream about it, whether you want to or not. Then, in the morning, we'll talk about your impressions."

Then he shut the library door before I could say another word.

I looked down at the card in my hands. I had gotten some vague homework assignments in my day, but this one just might take the cake. It almost made me miss my grandmother's freestyling teaching.

Almost.

I held the card in my teeth while I got back into all my winter gear, then trudged home to see what I could do with a Fe rune.

CHAPTER SIX

I TRIED to do as Haraldr asked me. I tried to meditate on the rune Fe, but nothing I did forged any feeling of connection within me.

I tried just sitting on the rug in front of my fireplace, the rune on its card resting on the floor in front of me, my eyes sort of focused on the flames of the fire as I settled into a deeper and deeper meditative state. But after more than an hour of that, I gave it up. Nothing was happening.

I ate a little lunch of toast and apple slices with honey, then went upstairs to see if taking a nap would help. I told myself this was because Haraldr had specifically mentioned dreams, but mainly it was just that after two nights of little sleep I was really tired.

When I got up again some time later, I felt rested, but had no memory of dreaming about anything in particular.

I got back into my coat and boots and headed outside to take a walk through the village. Haraldr had said I might find myself seeing the rune everywhere, but even when I was looking for things that reminded me of its shape, I saw nothing that struck any sort of magical resonance with me.

Still, I came home with a basket full of fresh food from the market-place, and I had chatted with several of my fellow Villmarkers, so the afternoon wasn't a complete waste. My Villmarker Norse was still far from fluent, but everyone was kind and perfectly willing to switch to English to help me out when I got stuck.

The sun was setting, and it was nearing dinnertime. I was tempted to head back to the mead hall and see if anyone was there, but in the end I decided not to. I needed to stick with my task, as futile as it felt. I looked over what I had bought at the market and decided to break out my ancestral cookware and make some potato soup.

The cooking felt normal enough. I had traded off that chore with my mother when she had been alive, and later with my grandmother down in Runde. I was no master chef, but I could make a range of basic meals. The routine felt normal. Homey.

But when I sat down at my table to eat with no one sitting across from me, that felt really weird. Like the house around me had suddenly gotten much larger, larger and emptier, its cavernous spaces echoing every scrape of my spoon against my bowl as I ate.

This was going to take some getting used to. It would help if Mjolner was there, but he had disappeared while I was talking with Haraldr and had yet to reappear.

Maybe he was in Runde visiting Jessica. That thought brought a stab to my heart, and I had to quickly push it away. Thinking of Jessica was going to lead to thinking about Andrew. And that would lead away from thinking about what I was here to do.

I drew a little Fe in the surface of my thick soup with the tip of my spoon and watched as it quickly filled back in. But even eating where it had been didn't make me feel closer to it. Not that I had expected it would.

After dinner I did the washing up, then went back into the great room. I looked at the cat bed, still empty. Then I wandered over to the south-facing windows. I looked down the slope of the hill, past the edges of the village proper to the low, rolling hills beyond.

I could just make out the trees that marked the location of Loke's house. I had yet to visit that house or meet his sister. I had neglected to ask about her when I had seen Loke the night before, but he had seemed in better spirits than he had been in for a long time. Surely that was a good sign. Perhaps I would meet her soon.

Finally, I turned away from the window and crossed the room to my art station. I clipped the card with the Fe drawing on it to the corner of my easel and looked at it for a moment. Then I looked over my supplies. Pen and ink seemed like the tools for this job. They were the ones I favored for my own work. I liked their unforgiving precision.

But after an hour or so, I had to admit I was *not* getting into my creative zone. I wasn't drawing the rune; I was just repeatedly writing it. I put the ink away and mulled over my supplies grumpily for a minute before taking out my largest tablet of paper and my charcoal.

I forced myself to see the rune as a collection of shapes and not like a letter I was trying to faithfully reproduce. It was not just another way of writing the letter F; it was something bigger.

I leaned into my work, using my fingertips and the sides of my hand to blend the charcoal as I drew the shapes that made Fe over and over again. This felt more like drawing than writing, at least. But the real creative zone was always just a little out of my reach.

Still, I persisted, filling page after page with dark, smudged drawings of overlapping Fe runes, large and small, backwards and forwards, right-side-up and upside-down.

I was vaguely aware that it had to be far past midnight. Weariness was starting to eat at the edges of my mind, and I knew that a third disrupted night's sleep wasn't going to be helpful at all.

But I felt so close to a breakthrough. Like my drawings were starting to almost get a little glow of magic to them. Magic that wasn't coming from me, but was being revealed by my efforts.

It was the crudest outlines of a sensation, but I was afraid to turn my attention to it properly, like examining it too closely would make it all fade away. So I just pushed my tiredness aside and kept drawing, hoping that feeling would get closer and stronger.

I don't know if that ever would've happened or if I was kidding myself. I didn't get a chance to really test it. Because my concentration was shattered in an instant by a scream.

A woman's scream. It tore apart the cold silence of the night like a sword slicing through an ice sculpture, leaving it all in pieces on the snowy ground.

And then, all too suddenly, it broke off, and the quiet of night came crashing back down like a pressure wave against my eardrums.

Someone was in trouble. And it might already be too late to help her.

I bolted for the door.

CHAPTER SEVEN

I THRUST my feet into my boots and grabbed my parka from its hook, but went out the door without putting it on or even tying my laces.

The night was colder than ever, my breath forming a thick fog that trailed behind me as I pushed my way past my garden gate and out into the street.

But then I stopped. I had no idea which way to go. Everything around me was so quiet and so still. No one else was coming outside to see what had happened. Had I imagined it? Had I touched on some magical thing while I had been drawing the rune?

No, that made no sense. Nothing about Fe suggested violence, and that scream had clearly been panicked. Then there was the fact that it had been cut off so abruptly. Someone had been hurt, or worse.

Suddenly I heard the slap of feet running. I stepped further out into the street, trying to pinpoint the direction.

They were running away from me, or at least from where I was standing, because the sound was definitely getting farther away, but I couldn't tell which way they were running. The echo up and down the house-lined streets just wouldn't let me even guess where the source was.

And then that sound, too, was gone. And I was alone, slowly

freezing in the icy air. I pulled on my parka, then took my hat and mittens out of its pockets.

I had no intention of going back inside until I knew what had happened, but where to start looking?

Suddenly there was a streak of motion, an inky black shadow racing against the backdrop of snow and icy cobblestones.

"Mjolner!" I cried. But he just ran past me without a glance, heading towards the square at the center of the village. I zipped up my parka as I ran, slipping on the ice and nearly tripping over my own bootlaces. I caught up with him at the well. He was walking all around it, rubbing his body against the stone sides and yowling loudly.

I gave him a reassuring pat on the head, then leaned over the side to look down into the well. I had never looked into it before, but I knew it was still a functioning well. There was water in there, but I had no idea how deep it had been dug to find it.

Even now I couldn't tell how deep it was, but I could see something reflecting starlight back up to me. Ice or water, it was too far away to be sure which.

Or if someone was down there in need of help. Or worse, beyond help.

I cast the one spell I knew best, a little spell to create a ball of light, then threw that light down into the well.

The glow from the light reflected off the icy sides of the well, then off the ice below. The ice was broken into floating pieces with water pooling on the tops of the larger pieces. Actively pooling; something had broken that ice just moments before.

There was also a dark shape down there, a shape that wasn't reflecting the light. A body? I couldn't tell, but it didn't seem to be moving.

And near the place where the ball of light had settled, there appeared to be a darker smear on the ice, already dissipating in that pooling water. Blood?

I straightened up and looked down at Mjolner, who was still behaving as if deeply upset.

"We need more help," I said to him, and he meowed back. I felt like he was telling me he was too shaken up to go on any missions. "It's okay, Mjolner. I've got this one."

Then I performed my second-best spell, the one that amplified my voice. No one else had heard that scream, apparently, but everyone was going to hear me.

"Villmarkers! Trouble in the commons!" I called out. I might have overdone it; I could hear the glass in the windows all around me rattling as the enhanced decibels of my voice shook them.

But it did the trick. Almost at once front doors were thrown open and people flooded out into the streets, all running to join me in the square.

"Ingrid! What is it?" a voice said behind me, and I spun around to see Thorbjorn and his brother Thorge at the head of the crowd coming down from the north end of town.

"Did no one hear that scream a moment ago?" I asked.

The two of them looked at each other before shaking their heads.

"We were awake in our kitchen, but we heard nothing," Thorge said.

"Where did you hear this scream?" Thorbjorn asked.

"I was at home, but I think it came from here," I said. "I think there's someone on the ice down in the well. But the ice is broken. They might sink before we get down there. How deep is it?"

"Deep," Thorbjorn said, and the two of them leaned over the side to look for themselves. I could see the silvery light of my spell on their faces as they leaned in a lot farther than I had tried to.

"She's right," Thorbjorn said, and Thorge nodded.

"Lower me down," he said, reaching for the rope tied to the winch over the well. Thorbjorn wrapped the bit closest to the winch around his waist, then handed the other end to his brother. Thorge bound it around his own waist, then threw both of his legs over the side of the well.

I almost yelped aloud, fearing he was going to plummet to the body, but he caught himself. He paused like that for a moment, hanging onto the stone lip by his fingertips. A look passed between him and Thorbjorn, and then he started climbing down, his body quickly blocking out the light from my spell.

"It's a woman," Thorge called up to us from the darkness below. "Blonde. I can't see her well enough to recognize her. There's a lot of blood."

"Is she alive?" I asked.

"Not breathing," he said between grunts. Thorbjorn braced himself more firmly, and I guessed Thorge had picked up the body. "I'm coming up," Thorge said.

The crowd around us was growing by the moment, but no one was coming closer. They just watched, some holding each other, a few whispering together. I scanned for familiar faces but didn't find any.

It was hard not to imagine that for at least one of them, it was because they were the one slung over Thorge's shoulder as he climbed. Could this be someone I knew?

Then someone else emerged from the crowd, pushing past the shocked villagers to reach us by the well. It was Thorbjorn's father, Valki. He gave me a solemn nod, then reached into the well to help Thorbjorn take the woman off of Thorge's shoulders.

They laid her gently on the cobblestones. Her blonde hair was loose but plastered to her face by icy water and blood. I dropped to my knees by her side and peeled off my mittens to touch her.

She was so cold already, and not breathing, and my fingers against the side of her neck felt no pulse.

I shook my head, although no one around me had asked if she was okay. I could feel that question just hanging over all of us, and I felt everyone's despair at my silent answer even more acutely.

I brushed the hair back from her face wet strand by wet strand. Thorbjorn was on his knees on the other side of the body, and his father and Thorge stood over us.

Thorbjorn must have recognized her first. I could hear the sharp intake of his breath, but before I could ask, I saw the freckle on her cheek.

"Sigvin?" I said, my hands shaking as I brushed back the last of her hair.

"No, not Sigvin," Thorge said. "It's her sister, Nefja."

He was right. My heart clenched in my chest. I had spent all last night in her company. She had been merry, laughing and teasing her sister, her cheeks bright in the too-warm mead hall, so full of life.

What was laying before me was like a shell of that woman, cold and empty. I wanted to find whoever was responsible for doing this to her, to make them pay for what they had taken out of the world.

But had it been a murder, or just a tragic accident?

I remembered the sound of feet running away, the only other person who had been around when I had first come outside.

I couldn't rest until I knew who that had been running away. And why. Had they fled the scene of a horrific accident? Or had they run to evade punishment for their crime?

CHAPTER EIGHT

I DIDN'T REALIZE how much I was projecting my outrage until I felt a hand on my shoulder, gently squeezing. I looked up at Thorbjorn, and he made a quick motion of his chin towards the crowd gathered around us.

They were stirring with the beginnings of anger. Had I done that?

I got to my feet and took a step or two away from Nefja's body. Thorbjorn stayed close at my side.

"You realize when you called us all out here, you put a panic inside all of our minds," he said to me in a low voice.

"No, I didn't know that. I didn't mean to. I didn't even know that was a thing I could do," I said.

"And now your anger is spreading like a virus," he said. "Can you calm your mind?"

I nodded, but it took more than a few deep breaths to release the tension in my whole body. I had to will my heart to stop pounding so furiously, to slow the rush of angry blood through my veins.

But when at last my hands unfisted, I sensed the people around me were calmer as well.

Was I amplifying things because of what I had been trying to do with the rune Fe? I had been so close to something, but then so abruptly interrupted. It felt a bit like I had run away from a bit of knitting with the yarn caught on me, unraveling it all over the place. Maybe that had set my magic haywire.

Or maybe it was just that I still didn't have very good control over my magic.

I would have to ask Haraldr about it in the morning.

"Nefja's family," I said. "Are they here?"

"I don't see them," Thorbjorn said. "Perhaps that's for the best. This isn't how they should find out what happened to her, to just find her lying on the street."

"What *did* happen to her?" I wondered aloud.

"There's just the one wound," Thorge said from where he had taken his brother's place, kneeling by Nefja's side. "Almost directly on top of her head. She must've fallen in somehow, toppled in head-first and hit the ice. I think she was probably gone in an instant."

"She fell in or was pushed," I murmured, but kept my feelings carefully clinical. "The scream I heard ended so quickly, I think you're right that she didn't linger after hitting the ice."

"Is that all you heard?" Thorbjorn asked.

"No, after I came out into the street it seemed to be completely quiet, but then I heard footsteps running away," I said. "I couldn't tell what direction they went. No one else was awake. I got the feeling that whoever was running knew I had come out. Like they were running from me."

"A feeling or a *feeling*?" Thorbjorn asked, raising one eyebrow.

I took a deep breath while I thought that over. "Just a feeling. The mundane kind. No magic."

"Perhaps just an odd coincidence, then," he said. "But we should investigate to be sure."

"I agree," I said.

Then he sighed. "But the first order of business is to go to Nefja's family. They must be told at once."

"I'll go with you," I said.

"Thorge and I will bring Nefja's body to Brigida's house for now," Valki said, and Thorbjorn nodded.

"Brigida has a room for such things," he whispered to me as Thorge picked up Nefja and placed her in his father's arms. "But the family will decide on what funeral rites to perform."

With the body gone, the crowd began to disperse. Thorbjorn and I blended in with other people going back to their homes, but by twos and threes they fell away until it was just the two of us heading south down the main road.

"Why would Nefja be out alone at this hour?" I asked. "It's long past midnight. And why would she be in the center of town?"

"Perhaps her sister can tell us more," Thorbjorn said.

Then he opened the garden gate in front of one of the houses and we walked up to the front door. Thorbjorn knocked softly, then a bit more briskly.

"I can try my voice again," I said.

"No, not unless you've figured out how to tone it down a little." There was a hint of teasing in his tone, but his eyes were worried. He knocked again, louder still, rattling the sturdy wooden door in its frame.

"You don't think something happened here as well?" I asked, my stomach sinking at the thought.

"I hope not," he said. But he was eyeing the door as if debating battering it down with his shoulder.

Then, finally, we heard footsteps approaching. Slow, shuffling, sleepy footsteps. At last the door opened and Sigvin, dressed in a long white flannel nightgown and fuzzy socks, blinked out at us.

"Wazzit?" she asked. Then her eyes seemed to finally focus on me. "Ingrid?"

"Sigvin. Are your parents home?" I asked.

"Yeah," she said, rubbing at her face as if to wake herself up. "Yes, they're upstairs."

"And they're all right?" Thorbjorn asked a little too forcefully.

She frowned at him with something like confusion in her eyes. I don't think she was awake enough yet to decide whether or not she should be worried. "I'm sure they're fine. Their room is at the back of the house, and they're both heavy sleepers. Why do you ask? Why are you here exactly?"

"I think we should go inside and sit down," I said. I aimed for my most gentle tone, but somehow my words ignited the panic in Sigvin that Thorbjorn's urgency had failed to.

"What's happened?" she demanded. Then her eyes went wide. "Is it Nefja? But no. She's sleeping in her room." She looked back over her shoulder as if she could see through walls and verify that this was true.

"Sigvin, let's sit down," I said. She turned back to look at me, her grip on the halfway-opened door so tight her knuckles were white and bloodless. But she shook her head.

"No, tell me here. Tell me now. What happened?"

"We don't exactly know how it happened," I said. "But I heard a scream a little while ago, and when I went out to investigate, I found your sister in the well. I'm sorry, Sigvin, but she's dead."

"But she's in her room," Sigvin said. Yet despite her own words of disbelief, I could see her eyes flooding with tears. "I put her to bed myself barely an hour ago. She was in no condition to get up again."

"She'd been drinking?" Thorbjorn asked.

"Yes, too much. That was my fault," she said. Then she pressed a hand to her mouth as horror filled her eyes. "It's all my fault, isn't it?"

"I doubt that very much," I said, but she dodged away from my attempts to touch her.

"You don't look like you've been drinking," Thorbjorn said.

"I had some mead. Not much," she said. "Nefja needed a little comfort, but I should have cut her off."

"What exactly happened last night?" Thorbjorn asked.

"It's a long story," she said, her voice still catching on random words. My heart was breaking for her. She was trembling as she stood in the doorway, looking back over one shoulder towards where I imagined her sister's bedroom must be and over the other towards the room of her still-sleeping parents.

"I think we need to hear it, Sigvin," Thorbjorn said.

"Right now?" I hissed at him.

"Sooner is better," he whispered back to me.

"I know, I know," Sigvin said. She pinched at the bridge of her nose for a moment, then took a deep breath. When she looked up at us again, she was the picture of calm resolve. "I know you need to hear the whole story. And I'll tell it to you, every detail I can remember, I swear it. But please, let me wake up my parents first and tell them what's happened. Alone?" she added with a hint of desperation.

Thorbjorn scowled, but I said, "of course we can wait until you've told your parents. It's not like you're a suspect," I added with a significant glance at Thorbjorn.

"Not a suspect?" Sigvin said. "You think this was a murder?"

"We think this was a murder?" Thorbjorn repeated. I realized I hadn't spoken any of my suspicions out loud to him yet.

"We don't know," I admitted to both of them.

"Well, if she was drinking as much as you say, perhaps not," Thorbjorn said. "Perhaps this was a tragic accident. But we need the whole story first."

"Murder," Sigvin said, fighting tears again. "Who would want to kill my sister?"

Then something dark passed over her face. She had not until that moment entertained such thoughts, but now that she had, I could tell she was starting to connect dots. She was coming up with a list of suspects. She was looking for motives and connections.

I knew those dark paths well.

"You're thinking something," Thorbjorn said.

"I am," she admitted. "But it would be easier to tell it all at once, from the beginning."

"After you talk to your parents," I said.

She nodded. Her lips twitched, not quite reaching the grateful smile I was sure she was trying for. But I nodded back my understanding.

"My father has taken Nefja to Brigida's house," Thorbjorn said. "You can go there to see her and speak with Brigida about what you will have done."

"Of course. Thank you," Sigvin said.

"Then, when you're ready, come to my house," I said. "We'll be waiting for you there. I would like to hear your version of events as soon as possible."

"I want you to hear what happened from me first, that's for sure," Sigvin said. "I'll be there as soon as I can."

"Are you sure you don't want us to stay?" I asked.

"No, I would prefer to do this alone. Just the family," she said. "But thank you, Ingrid. I know you will find out what really happened to my sister. I have complete faith in that."

She reached out and clasped my hand, just one quick squeeze, and then she stepped back and shut the door.

I looked up at Thorbjorn and realized that the sun must be close to rising, as I could see him more clearly now.

He looked down at me with sadness in his eyes.

"What is it?" I asked. That sadness felt too personal to be about Nefja.

"This is not how I would've chosen to welcome you to your new home," he said.

"I know," I said.

Although personally, I thought it felt entirely appropriate. Investigating a suspicious death? That was what the two of us did.

I was just grateful that for once at least this case didn't seem likely to cross the boundary between Villmark and Runde.

Of course, we had no suspects or clues yet. Who could know where this all would lead to in the end?

CHAPTER NINE

As we walked up the road towards my house, we could see the well standing alone in the center of the commons at the top of the hill silhouetted against the graying sky.

"Tell me about these footsteps," Thorbjorn said.

"There's nothing more to tell," I said. "They came and went so quickly. I was the only one outside, or at least it felt that way. And the air had a strange quality to it. You know how when it's really cold it feels like sound can just travel forever? And it's not like being in a fog, where every sound is like it's coming from all around you. No, in the cold air it's more like everything you hear is the same volume, near or far, and you can hear things from so very far away. Do you know what I mean?"

"A bit," he said, but pressed on for more concrete information. "You said before you couldn't tell the direction, but what about other clues? Like, how heavy was the tread? Would you guess that it was a man or a woman?"

"I really couldn't say," I said with a sigh. "It was over before I could really properly listen."

"Is it possible there was more than one person? Perhaps two running together?"

"Is that likely?" I asked. "No, I'm pretty sure it was just one person. But beyond that, I don't know."

He grunted. I wasn't sure what that sound meant, but at least we were standing at my garden gate now.

"You're coming in, right?" I asked.

"Absolutely," he said. "I want to be here when Sigvin tells her tale."

"I'll get some coffee going, then," I said. I knew I must be craving it something fierce, because I could almost smell it brewing already. I shed my outer layers, then went into the kitchen.

And came to an abrupt halt in the doorway. There were already people in my kitchen. "Nilda. Kara."

"Ingrid," Nilda said, getting up from the table to pull me into a tight hug.

"You've heard about Nefja," I guessed.

"We heard," Kara said.

"We let ourselves in. I hope that's okay?" Nilda said.

"We figured you were working the case already, and that you'd appreciate coffee and rolls when you got back," Kara said. She looked as glum as her sister, although she perked up a little when Thorbjorn appeared in the doorway.

"Rolls?" he asked.

"Cinnamon rolls," Nilda said. "We just put them in the oven, but they'll be ready shortly."

Now that I knew I wasn't imagining the coffee smell in the air, I realized I had also been smelling cinnamon as well as yeasty bread. And just like that, my mouth was watering.

"You guys are working together again?" Kara asked with a feigned casual air. "The inseparable pair are on the case."

"Yes, indeed," Thorbjorn said. "We're waiting for Sigvin to come and tell us what happened last night."

"What do you mean last night? Not early this morning?" Nilda asked.

"Sigvin wasn't there when it happened, was she?" Kara asked. "That's not what we heard. We heard Nefja fell in the well, but if no one raised an alarm, she must have been alone."

"I didn't think it could be an accident," Nilda said, hugging herself tightly. "I wanted to think it was, but I just didn't. It didn't make any sense, Nefja out alone in the middle of the night just falling into the well. But her being out in the middle of the night getting murdered doesn't make any sense either."

"Sigvin said Nefja had been drinking," I said.

Nilda and Kara traded a glance.

"Yes, she had definitely been drinking," Nilda said. I waited for her to go on, but instead she turned to the coffeepot and filled a mug for Thorbjorn and another for me. I put my face over the mouth of my mug, letting the rich roasted smell of the coffee and the heat of the steam both wash over my face before taking a sip.

"You two were there as well," Thorbjorn said as he accepted the other mug from Nilda's hands.

"At the mead hall we were at the other night?" I guessed.

"The same," Nilda said, sliding back into the chair she had been sitting in before. Thorbjorn and I joined her and Kara at the table.

"Did anything strange or remarkable happen besides the drinking?" Thorbjorn asked.

"It didn't seem so at the time," Kara said.

"Just tell it all from the beginning," I suggested. "Something that seems minor now could be important later when we have more leads, so don't leave anything out."

"Okay," Nilda said, glancing at her sister.

"You tell it," Kara said. "I'll pipe in if there's anything I want to add."

"Okay," Nilda said again, pressing her palms flat on the surface of my table. I could see she was reluctant to start, or unsure where to begin, but I said nothing. Eventually she came to a decision and with a little nod began her tale.

"When Kara and I came in, it was about dinnertime for us. Which is early for most, so it wasn't weird that the only customer in the place was Roarr. He was eating alone, sort of."

"Sort of?" I asked.

"He didn't have anyone at the table with him," she said. "But that server, Bera... do you know her?" I shook my head. "She was there the night we all were there. But she's kind of quiet, so I'm not surprised you don't remember her. She just brought us our food and refilled our cups. She's not one for chatting with the customers."

"She likes Roarr," Kara said. "He always gets extra on his plate, and she's super attentive to keeping his cup full. You must have noticed that."

I cast my mind back to our evening together. I remembered meatballs and mashed vegetables and more kinds of little cubes of cheese than I could identify.

Then I also remembered how Roarr, who had been sitting between me and Loke, always had more food than the rest of us. I hadn't really noticed that server, aside from thinking to myself that she seemed awfully tiny to be schlepping so much food around.

"Did Roarr do anything?" Thorbjorn asked.

"No, he was just eating by himself, perfectly content," Nilda said. "Or he was until we came in, because Sigvin and Nefja came in right behind us."

"Nefja was never subtle about her feelings for Roarr," Thorbjorn said.

"That's putting it mildly," Kara said.

"So did something happen?" I asked.

"Not that we saw," Nilda said. "But Kara and I weren't there long. I mean, Nefja was clearly trying to catch Roarr's eye, but she never managed it. He just focused on his food, and on Beer bringing him the food."

"I think he was ignoring Nefja on purpose," Kara put in.

"And for her part, Sigvin was preoccupied with the possibility that Loke might make another appearance," Nilda said. "It was a little lonely eating dinner with a bunch of companions all looking elsewhere." Her eyes made a quick darting glance to her sister, and I knew with perfect clarity that Nilda wasn't just talking about Sigvin and Nefja being distracted. Her own sister had been watching for someone special to arrive as well. But Nilda had no intention of outing her sister in front of her crush, so I said nothing either.

"Did Loke show up?" Thorbjorn asked.

"Not while we were there," Nilda said. "But we didn't stay long. Nefja was clearly determined to make Roarr notice her, and Sigvin was sort of giving in to that impulse. Like she was willing to sit up with her sister all night if that's what it took."

"Especially if Loke might stop by later," Kara said then took a sip of coffee.

"Yes. Well. I don't know," Nilda said in a primly diplomatic tone.

"We left early," Kara said, clearly a gesture to get the story back on track.

"Yes, we only stayed to eat, and then we went home," Nilda said. "I don't know that we saw anything that I would call suspicious exactly. But Nefja was definitely in a high energy mood. Keyed up. When we left, I remember feeling a little bad for Roarr. Because I was sure after another mug of ale or two, she'd be demanding he declare his feelings for her."

"Feelings he doesn't have," Kara said.

"Which would just be awkward for everyone involved," Nilda said.

"Is that why you left early?" I asked.

She flushed in embarrassment, and I knew the answer was yes.

"We should talk to Loke and Roarr," Thorbjorn said to me.

"Are they suspects?" Kara asked.

"We don't even know for sure that it's a murder yet," I admitted. "And anyway, why Loke?"

"Well, just to be thorough, we should get their sides of the story," he said.

"But we don't even know if Loke was there," I said.

"When we talk to him, we can find that out," Thorbjorn said, a little too perfectly reasonably.

"Do you want us to help?" Kara asked eagerly. "If you two are waiting here for Sigvin, Nilda and I can go find Roarr and Loke and tell them to come here and talk to you as well."

"That would be helpful," Thorbjorn agreed.

"Sure," I said.

"Keep an eye on those rolls," Nilda said as she got up from the table. "They'll be done when they're golden brown, probably five more minutes?"

"Got it," I said as I walked with her and her sister to the front door. "Thanks for doing that, by the way."

"Just our contribution to the pursuit of justice," she said. Then they each gave me another hug before heading out into the early morning street.

The snow was already blinding. Or perhaps the sudden jabbing pain in my head was not from the light but from yet another morning with too much caffeine and too little sleep.

When my front door closed, I turned but headed out to the great room rather than the kitchen. I crossed to my easel to pick up the shattered remains of the charcoal stick I had dropped hours before. Then I looked at the overlapping runes like tumbling ghost shapes against the darkness of the charcoal. What I had been doing looked more like a negative image of a drawing than an actual drawing, like I had formed the shapes by removing charcoal rather than adding it.

It was eerie, but it didn't have any magical glow in my eyes. But I must have unleashed something. I had been spilling my emotions over onto half the town without even realizing it. I had it under control now, but I hadn't before.

Had I made this whole thing happen? Had I been putting out some sort of energy across the whole sleeping village? Had it affected Nefja and the person who had been running away?

I didn't like that feeling at all. But my logical brain insisted that it was probably a coincidence, that I had been drawing when the accident happened. It didn't feel like I had caused anything.

But it hadn't felt like I was emotionally controlling the crowd either.

With a sigh, I headed back to the kitchen with the broken bits of charcoal in my hand. My nose was telling me it was time to take those rolls out of the oven, and that was one sense I knew I could still rely on.

CHAPTER TEN

I HAD JUST TAKEN the rolls out of the oven when there was a tentative knock on my front door. It was so soft I thought at first I might have imagined it, but Thorbjorn got up and briefly made eye contact with me before heading out to the hall. I set the pan on a trivet and pulled off my oven mitt before following behind him.

I felt something brush past my legs and realized that Mjolner was back. He was moving past me as if he had just come in through the front door. The front door Thorbjorn hadn't even opened yet. I turned to watch him head into the great room and zip over to his bed by the fireplace. Then I turned back to step up behind Thorbjorn as he opened the door.

Sigvin was standing red-eyed on the front step, her hand raised as if to knock again. She pulled her hand back, twisting it up with her other mittened hand as if she were in the height of anxiety.

"Come in," Thorbjorn said, stepping back to let her into the mudroom. She came in, then wavered uncertainly before pulling off her mittens and starting to unbutton her heavy wool coat.

"How are your parents doing?" I asked.

"As well as can be expected," Sigvin said. "I told them I would join them at Brigida's house when I'm done here."

"I don't think we'll keep you long," I said, glancing over at Thorbjorn.

"It depends on what she has to say," he told me.

"Of course," Sigvin said as she hung up her coat, then slipped out of her boots.

"Come into the kitchen," I said to her. "I'll pour you a cup of coffee, and you can have a cinnamon roll if you like."

I had a sudden flash of memory, of that first day after my mother had passed. She had been sick for a long time before, in fact for most of my life, but it had still felt jarringly sudden when she was gone. I couldn't imagine how Sigvin felt, losing a twin with no warning. I was sure that coffee and cinnamon rolls would be of no real help, but it was all I had. And when it had been me in the first stages of grief, I don't think I would've eaten at all if people hadn't kept foisting food onto me. I hadn't tasted a bit of it, but it had kept me alive, I suppose.

Sigvin took the mug of coffee from me, then set it down untasted on the table in front of her. I plated up one of the steaming hot rolls and set it in front of her as well, but she didn't even seem to notice.

"Where should I start?" she asked as Thorbjorn and I sat down across from her.

"At the beginning," Thorbjorn said. Sigvin seemed to find this answer distressing, and I couldn't blame her. On top of everything, she was supposed to figure out where the beginning had been?

"We know that you went to the mead hall for dinner. That you and Nefja met Nilda and Kara there," I said.

"Yes," Sigvin said. "It was going to be just the four of us, catching up on things." Her cheeks flushed a dark pink and her fingers started pulling bits off the cinnamon roll, and I suspected what the four of them had been catching up on was perhaps related to me and my sudden move into the village and what it might meant for them.

They had wanted to talk about me when I wasn't there. Perfectly natural, and yet a little strange to hear about after the fact.

"Was going to be," Thorbjorn repeated. "That isn't what happened?"

"Well, when we got there, Roarr was already there," she said, still looking at the roll she was breaking to bits. "I guess you already know that Nefja has... had a thing for Roarr."

"Lots of women do, since Lisa passed," Thorbjorn observed.

"I suppose," Sigvin said. "Maybe she wasn't more obsessed than the others, I don't know. But she was my sister, and this new fixation she had on Roarr was hard for me to grasp, I think."

"What do you mean?" I asked.

"It was so sudden and so strong," Sigvin said. "I sometimes thought... but no. Never mind."

"You thought someone was doing some magic?" Thorbjorn guessed.

"Roarr has no talent for magic that I've ever seen," I assured her.

"I know. But he was with Halldis for a long time. And she gave him at least one charm. There might have been others," she said.

I glanced over at Thorbjorn in alarm. Was this possible?

"His home was searched by the council, myself, and Nora Torfudottir," he said, which was news to me. 'He had nothing of the sort still in his possession. We made sure of this."

"And I've been near the two of them before, Nefja and Roarr," I said. "If something magical was flowing between them, I would've seen it."

Sigvin sighed. "That might've been a comfort to know, yesterday."

"Do you think Roarr had something to do with this?" I asked, but Thorbjorn raised a hand.

"Please, no conjecture or accusations. Not yet. Just tell us what happened last night," he said.

Sigvin nodded her understanding. "We ate dinner, the four of us. Nefja was very worked up. She was clearly trying to get Roarr's attention, but he never noticed her. The only person he even looked up at was the serving girl who was bringing him more food."

"Did he seem preoccupied?" Thorbjorn asked.

"Not particularly. Just hungry, I guess," Sigvin said. "So the four of us finished dinner, and Nilda and Kara went home. Kara was looking for someone who never turned up, and Nilda was just done for the night, I guess." Her cheeks were coloring again, but if Thorbjorn noticed, he said nothing.

"You and Nefja stayed to drink?" I asked.

"Well, not like that," she said. "I mean, it wasn't my intention to let my sister get smashed. We were just going to have a mug of ale by the fire. I didn't think I was going to get her out of there before Roarr left, and it looked like he was nearly done eating, so I was just playing for time."

"Did he leave?" Thorbjorn asked.

"Eventually, but that's not what happened next," Sigvin said. "Someone else came in."

"Loke?" I guessed.

She looked surprised I would mention him. Then she was flushing guiltily again. "No. Well, eventually yes, but at that moment no. It was a crowd of the men who usually drink at Aldís' mead hall at the western edge of town. Thorbjorn knows the one I mean."

"I do too, actually," I said. And I could imagine the sort of men she meant. The men I had met when I had been there had been very much against mixing with people not from Villmark. They hadn't liked me much, but they had liked Loke, Nilda and Kara little more. Not only did they not like people outside of Villmarkers, they didn't like Vill-markers who associated with non-Villmarkers either.

Which would make the mead hall by the gardens a very odd choice for their nightly libations.

"Names?" Thorbjorn asked.

"Báfurr. Raggi. Skefill. A few others I didn't recognize," she said.

"I've met Raggi," I said to Thorbjorn.

"I know the others," he said to me. Then to Sigvin, "any idea why they were at Ullr's place? It's not their usual hangout."

Sigvin sighed again, but her breath wavered this time, as if a sob might be in the offing. But she held it back. Her eyes were glassy but without tears. "They were there because of Nefja."

Thorbjorn and I both sat up straighter at the same time. This sounded like a proper lead at last.

"Why?" Thorbjorn asked.

"One of them, Báfurr, is infatuated with her," Sigvin said. "We used to go to Aldís' hall from time to time, the two of us, just for a change. Her mead is quite good, and she roasts elk like no one else. But we got a lot of attention there. Not many single women go there. At first it was nice, you know, but it got to be a bit too much. I got tired of it first, but I stayed anyway, not to be the one who spoils things, you know? But as with most things, once Nefja was done with that place, that was it. She doesn't change her mind once she's made it. I don't think we'd ever have gone back there. So I guess they came looking for us. Or rather, Báfurr brought the others around in search of Nefja."

"So there was a confrontation?" I asked.

"No, at first they played it like they were just there to drink together," Sigvin said. "They sat near us, but not obnoxiously so. I know they were watching us, but they weren't being aggressive with it. I figured Roarr would finish his food, then Nefja could finish her ale, and we'd go home."

"But?" I prompted.

"But that serving girl kept bringing Roarr more and more food. I don't know how he was packing it all in or why he didn't tell her to stop already, but he didn't. And Nefja's ale was gone, and before I could say anything she was ordering another."

"Two ales isn't so bad," I said.

"Well, halfway through the second was when she started to talk," Sigvin said, flushing embarrassedly again.

"To whom?" Thorbjorn asked.

"Well, I suppose to me, but it was more like she was ranting to the whole room," she said. "I mean, she wanted Roarr to hear her, I'm sure, but in the process she was announcing to everyone in the hall that she was fed up with waiting around and either she was going to end the evening with a more formal sort of attachment or she'd be giving it up all together."

"How did Roarr take that?" Thorbjorn asked.

"He didn't even seem to hear her," Sigvin shrugged. "But Báfurr most certainly did. And he came over to sit right next to Nefja. He took her hand and tried to plead his case. He'd done that before, at Aldís' place. But he's an old-fashioned guy. He was all about what he had and what he could offer her in terms of comfort and a good solid house, that sort of thing."

"Not what Nefja was looking for," I guessed.

"Well, it's not like she doesn't want all that," Sigvin said. Then her voice choked as she corrected herself. "Didn't. It's not like she didn't want that. But she didn't want to marry just for material things. But Báfurr doesn't have a romantic bone in his body. I don't think he could tell her what she wanted to hear in a million years, because I don't think it ever occurred to him that she would want to hear something else. Something about her beauty or glowing personality or anything besides what a good breeder of sons she might be."

"So she rebuked him?" I guessed.

"She didn't mean to be harsh," Sigvin said. "But she's let him down gently so many times before, and she was at the bottom of that second ale now. She was a bit blunter than she needed to be, and I could see he was angry at her words. But he didn't say anything in return, just went back to his friends. He could tell as well as I that she had had too much to drink. Words spoken in such circumstances can be forgiven in the morning, right?"

"It depends on the person, and on the words," Thorbjorn said.

"What happened then?" I asked.

"Then," Sigvin said with another shaky inhale of breath, "she ordered a third ale. And after a single swig of that, she crossed the room to throw herself on Roarr's lap."

Thorbjorn tried to bite back a laugh, but didn't quite succeed. "Sorry. But I bet Roarr couldn't ignore her then."

"No, he could not," Sigvin said. "And she was still talking. Words I knew she would die of embarrassment if she even remembered speaking them in the morning. Roarr looked frankly alarmed, like he didn't know how to get rid of her. He didn't want to touch her, but he couldn't get her off his lap without doing so. And I was at loose ends as well. I was afraid if I tried to pull her away that she'd start making a real scene and neither of us would be welcome back ever again."

"It was that bad?" I asked, wincing a little in empathy.

"It was that bad," she agreed, but then she brightened a little. "And then Loke was there. He came in the door, looked around, and it was like he knew at once everything that was going on. He saw me, hovering uselessly, and Nefja driving Roarr out of his mind with embarrassment. I think he even saw Báfurr watching everything with a glower as he nursed his own anger.

"He took all that in, and then came down the steps and caught Nefja by her hand and just twirled her up off of Roarr's lap and into his own arms, like he wanted to dance with her. He spun her around and around, and I was a bit worried that she might get sick on him. But she just grinned like it was all a mad game. Meanwhile Loke keeps hissing at Roarr out of the corner of his mouth to run out of there.

"But Roarr just sat there like he was paralyzed. I had to get him to his feet and herd him out the back door, through the kitchens. Once he was outside, it was like the cold air just snapped him awake. He ran off towards his house, shouting his thanks back to me."

I glanced over at Thorbjorn, but he was listening to Sigvin's story too intently to notice me.

"Was that the last of it?" I asked.

"Sadly, no," Sigvin said. "I went back inside to find that Loke and Nefja had stopped dancing. He had put her into a chair, and at first I thought that was for the best. But then I saw that Báfurr was there again, talking to her. I tried to run to her, but the room had gotten a lot more crowded, and I had to push my way past too many people. I was too late. When I got there, she was giving Báfurr an even more explicit piece of her mind, and this time his face was so flushed with anger it was practically purple. I won't repeat what she said, but her contempt for him and everything he was offering her was very, very clear."

"What did he do?" I asked.

"In that moment, nothing," she said. "He went back to his friends yet again, and I pleaded with Loke to help me get her home before she started talking again or worse get ahold of another mug of ale."

"So Loke and you got Nefja home and in bed," I said.

"I don't think I could've done it without him. He was a lifesaver," she said. Then she seemed to hear her own words, and the color drained from her face. The corners of her eyes were starting to twitch, and I didn't think she was going to succeed in fighting back the tears this time.

"Loke is a good man," Thorbjorn said, words I never thought I'd ever hear him say. But they had a calming effect on Sigvin.

"That he is," she agreed. Her eyes were still sad, but they were more wistful than grieving now. "But that's the end of my story. I put Nefja to bed in her room. She was already out of it, I really don't know how she could've gotten up again, and that's the truth. I went to bed myself and was asleep before my head even hit the pillow. Well, you your-selves know how many times you had to knock to wake me. And I was nowhere near as bad off as Nefja was."

"When Loke left your house, did you see which way he went?" Thorbjorn asked.

Sigvin frowned. "I don't know that I remember," she said. "I did invite him to stay, since it was so late and so cold that night. We have a spare room, you know. But he turned me down. He said he had to get home to his sister." Then she put her fingers over her eyes. At first I was afraid she was breaking down again, but when she dropped her hands again, I realized she had only been doing that as a way to focus on her memory. "He left through an alley," she said. "Going north. Not towards his house, but not towards Roarr's either."

"Towards the well in the center of town?" I asked.

"Well, that *is* north of us, but there are more direct ways to get there than down the alleyways," she said.

"You never heard the scream?" Thorbjorn asked. "Or the door opening and closing when your sister left?"

"I barely heard you two knocking," she said, shaking her head. "I don't want to think about someone deliberately hurting my sister, but I can't imagine her getting up again and going out. And to do it so quietly I didn't hear it?" She shook her head again.

"It's a mystery," I said.

"Are you sure it wasn't an accident?" she asked.

"I'm not sure of anything yet," I admitted.

"Well, I'm sure of one thing," Sigvin said, raising her chin defiantly. "I'm sure that whatever happened, you'll get to the bottom of it. I know that deep in my bones."

I didn't know what to say to that. Thank her? I was nowhere near as confident as she was.

Apologize in advance for letting her down?

I started to open my mouth, still not sure what words I was going to summon, but Thorbjorn stopped me by resting a hand on my knee under the table. While I was too startled by his touch to speak, he said, "thank you, Sigvin. You may join your parents now, with our condolences. We'll let you know if we have any further questions."

"Of course," she said. Her eyes darted from him to me and back again, but she left without saying a word.

CHAPTER ELEVEN

I LISTENED to the sounds of Sigvin getting back into her winter things. I was waiting to hear the sound of the door closing behind her before asking Thorbjorn what he thought of her story, but I didn't get my chance. I heard the door open, but then there was a murmur of voices. Sigvin was talking to someone who had been standing outside my door.

I went into the hallway and saw Roarr halfway up my front walk, his wool hat in his hands as he looked up at Sigvin. Her back was rigid, and her gloved hands were in fists.

"Is everything all right?" I asked.

"I was just expressing my condolences to Sigvin here," Roarr said. "I have, of course, heard the news."

"What good to me are your condolences?" she spat at him.

"Sigvin!" I gasped. I rushed to her side to put a hand on her arm before she did anything violent. I had never seen her angry before, not even annoyed. But now she was incandescent with sudden rage.

"It is all I have to offer you," Roarr said, shifting from foot to foot.

"You never loved my sister," she said, blinking furiously.

"No, I did not," he admitted. "I told her as much over and over again. I'm sorry that she could never hear it. But I know what it's like to lose someone you love, to lose them suddenly, to be unmoored. I am sorry for your pain. Yours and your parents.'"

Then all the tension washed out of Sigvin's body in a rush, and I put a hand on her elbow to keep her from collapsing to the floor.

"I'm the one who's sorry," she said. "You're right. You never led my sister on. She just never heard you, or me either, for that matter. Thank you for your kind words. Now, if you'll excuse me, I really should get back to my parents."

He nodded, stepping aside so she could walk down the steps to the garden path without physically brushing past him.

"Let me know if you need anything from me," I called after her. "Anything at all."

"I will," she promised before letting herself out of the garden gate.

Then she was gone, and it was just me and Roarr.

"Come in," I said to him, suddenly very tired. I doubted today I would have any time for naps.

I led Roarr into the kitchen where Thorbjorn had already poured him a cup of coffee. The smell perked me up, if only a little, and I slid back into my own seat and took a sip from the mug Thorbjorn must've freshened up while I was in the front hall.

"You don't honestly believe I had anything to do with this," Roarr said, leaning forward over the table to be sure I would meet his eyes.

"I don't want to," I admitted. "But we'd still like to hear your version of the events of last night."

"In as much detail as you can recall," Thorbjorn said as he took his seat beside me.

Roarr nodded and took another sip of coffee. "My parents are at our hunting lodge, so I'm home alone at the moment. When they are gone, I generally prefer to eat out rather than fix meals for just me. And Ullr has the best meatballs in Villmark, so I tend to dine there."

"This was true the other night as well," I guessed.

"Yeah. What did you think, that I go out just to get swarmed by desperate women?" He scoffed a humorless laugh at his own expense.

"Well," I drawled. He scowled at me. "Normally I'd suspect it, but clearly that's not who you are. We've covered this territory before, you and I."

"I should say we have," he said.

"So you were eating alone. And early, I take it?" I asked.

"After Loke had to save me the night you were there, it seemed better to eat early and leave before the place got crowded," he said. "I would've made it earlier still if I knew who was going to show up for an early supper of their own."

"You were avoiding Nefja?" I guessed.

"As much as I can," he admitted. "She's a lovely young woman, really, but lately she's been trying to put more and more pressure on me. I don't want to be rude to her, but she doesn't hear me when I'm polite, I guess."

"She's not the only one who's been trying to get your attention," I said.

"Well, no," he said. "But most women are subtler about it. They don't stop by my house with baskets of things I don't need, or sneak personal messages into my very bedroom when I'm not there, or try to win my mother over to their side."

"Was Nefja doing that?" Thorbjorn asked, clearly horrified.

"Yeah," Roarr said, peering into his coffee mug before taking another swallow.

"That's... wow," Thorbjorn said, shaking his head. "Maybe you should spend more time with me and my brothers."

"Maybe," Roarr said with half a smile. "I notice none of you are married, and yet none of you have this hangers-on problem."

"It's complicated," Thorbjorn said.

"And perhaps a bit off topic?" I interjected. Because it was, but because there was no way I could listen to that conversation, not knowing that Thorbjorn at least did have someone pining for him. Just because he hadn't noticed her didn't mean she wasn't there.

And I kind of suspected that was true of his brothers as well. All of them were excessively easy on the eyes.

"Right," Roarr said. "So Sigvin and Nefja came in when I was still the only one there, but then Nilda and Kara came in right after.

Usually the three of them, Sigvin plus the Mikkelsen sisters, are enough to keep Nefja in check, so I didn't panic. I intended to quietly finish my meal and then make myself scarce, hopefully after the hall had started to fill up when my escape might go unnoticed.

"But that's not what happened. Sigvin seemed distracted, constantly looking towards the door like she was waiting for someone, and when she wasn't looking Nefja was downing ales like she was in a drinking contest. She was putting away a lot more than her sister noticed, that's for sure. Then Kara and Nilda left, but Sigvin and Nefja didn't. I have no idea why. But Nefja had a very aggressive energy, even for her."

"In what way?" Thorbjorn asked.

"Oh, just looks and I guess flirting or whatever," Roarr said. "I ignored her, but ignoring her just seemed to wind her up more. I admit I was a little worried that the point of all that ale was to give her a little liquid courage."

"To go talk to you?" I asked.

"But she was already direct with you, right?" Thorbjorn said. "No liquid courage required."

"I know," Roarr said. "It was more like she was building to a final showdown. And I lingered, because while half of me wanted to run away, the other half just wanted to get it all over with. I confess I knew harsh words would likely be necessary, but I hoped whatever I said she wouldn't remember exactly later. I mean, I hoped she remembered the thrust of my words. That she would finally give up pursuing me."

"But you didn't approach her to say any of this," I said.

"No, because of that other half of me that still wanted to run away," he said. His cheeks colored just a little. "And then the isolationists came in. You know who I mean. The Aldís crowd."

"Specifically who?" Thorbjorn asked.

"Oh, the usual ones. Báfurr for sure. A few others from his particular group. Raggi. I think Skefill. But they favor cloaks with deep hoods that they keep over their faces, you know?"

"Indeed," Thorbjorn agreed.

"Nefja was talking too loudly by that point, pretending to talk about the inadequacies of men in general but clearly speaking to me," Roarr said. "But then Báfurr crossed the room to sit beside her. I didn't hear what he said to her, but we all heard her reject him."

"And how did he take it?" I asked.

"Given her words, which were unnecessarily harsh, better than I would've thought," Roarr said. "He just slinked back to his friends and resumed drinking with them. But Nefja was even more charged up than before now, and she came over to me. She just plopped herself down on my lap. And I was just frozen. I wanted her off of me, but I really didn't want to have to touch her. I was hoping Sigvin would intervene, but she didn't."

"You were embarrassed," I said.

"Well, yeah," he admitted. "But then Loke came in and saw at once what was going on. He pulled Nefja off of my lap and kept her distracted while the server, that tiny girl, helped me sneak out through the kitchen. Now I owe him one."

"Because he saved you?" I asked.

"At risk to himself, you know," Roarr said. "I could already see Sigvin closing in on him. She might carry herself with more dignity than her sister, but she's still deeply smitten with Loke and not afraid to show it."

"I've seen how he runs from that," I said. Although I wasn't sure why. It always felt a touch extreme. Sigvin would never do anything to embarrass him. Why flee from a little quiet admiration?

"So you went straight home?" Thorbjorn asked.

"Not right away," Roarr said. "I needed a walk to clear my head. I hadn't said any of the words I had been prepared to say, and I needed to decide what I was going to do about that. Because ignoring her was clearly no longer going to work."

"How long were you walking?" I asked. "Through what parts of town?"

"Through all the parts," he said. "And I was still out walking when I heard that scream." He shuddered. "It was so shrill, but ended so abruptly. It was absolutely chilling."

"You heard Nefja scream?" I asked. "I thought only I had heard that."

"It carried through the streets, but I couldn't tell from where. I kept walking, hoping I'd hear something more, but I never figured out where it was coming from until I came upon the crowd gathered around the well."

"That was some time later," I said.

"It was," he nodded. "I went up and down a lot of streets looking for signs of trouble."

"Did you see any?" Thorbjorn asked.

"Not a one."

"Did you see anyone else out on the streets?" I asked.

"No."

"Did you hear anyone else? Like footsteps walking or running?"

"Not a thing," he said. "I know that means I have no alibi. But I've told you everything. I know you'll never stop until you find the truth, and I have faith in that. Because I know *you* know I'd never harm anyone for the lowly crime of embarrassing me."

Thorbjorn shifted in his seat, covering his face with his hand and half-looking away, and I realized those last words had been directed more at him than me. As if Roarr had read his mind and knew he had been thinking of just such a motive.

"You are correct that I will do all I can to solve this crime," I said.

"I want to help in any way I can," he said. "I know I still have work to do to redeem myself in the eyes of others and even being a witness, let alone a suspect to this, isn't going to help."

"I understand," I said, glancing over at Thorbjorn. He looked back at me, clearly communicating that he wasn't going to be shamed for suspecting Roarr.

Then I turned back to Roarr. "There is something you can do for me," I said.

"Anything," he said, getting to his feet as if to prove how swiftly he would undertake any task.

"I need someone to go to Haraldr's house and explain that I won't be there for my lesson this morning," I said. "I need to follow up on a few more things before I can get back to my studies. I hope he'll understand."

"I'll see that he does," Roarr said. The look on his face was so earnest I almost wished I could've given him some noble quest to carry out instead.

But calling in sick for me was the most I had for him to do.

CHAPTER TWELVE

I turned to Thorbjorn. "Let's break this down," I said. "You really think Roarr is a suspect?"

"Everyone is a suspect," he said.

"You know, that's never actually true," I said. "There are always people you can rule out straight away. No opportunity, no motive, no means."

"Roarr hasn't been ruled out by any of those," Thorbjorn said. "In fact, if we're talking about who would be capable of throwing Nefja over the wall and down into that well, that really narrows our list of suspects by a lot. And Roarr would still be on that list."

"What do you mean?" I asked.

"Assuming it wasn't an accident, assuming that she was pushed into that well, it would take someone of some strength to accomplish it," he said. "You saw it took my brother, father, and I working together to get her back out of it."

I remembered the stone wall of the well. It was about four feet high. Taller than my waist, not so tall as my armpits. Nefja was a little taller than me, but not much.

"How could it have been an accident, then?" I asked.

"If she saw something and was reaching in," he said. "That's the only way. She didn't trip and fall in there, that's for sure. On the other hand, throwing her in there would've been a lot of work. Even if there was more than one person attacking her and they could work quickly, she would still have screamed more."

"It didn't sound like she screamed until she fell into the well," I said. "It was short."

"If Roarr had been with her, she would've been calm. She would've trusted him. Right up until the minute he pushed her in. Assuming it was him, of course," he said. Then he got up from the table to gather empty coffee cups and carry them to the sink.

"I can do that later," I said. "I want to talk to you now."

He sighed, looking out my kitchen window to the eastern sky. "I know you do, but I have to go take care of some things first."

"What kinds of things?" I asked.

"Thor things," he said in a tone clearly meant to encourage me to drop it.

"You can't be serious," I said. I was getting too close to knowing how Nefja felt with Roarr running out the back door to avoid her, and I didn't like it.

"Ingrid, you know I have responsibilities," he said. "I've been here long enough. My brothers are waiting for me, and it's getting late."

"So I'm on my own with this investigation now?" I asked.

He sighed then laughed, a strange combination. "Look," he said. "First of all, you being on your own has never stopped you solving things before, so don't look at me like that. Second of all, if you say Roarr should not be on our list of suspects, I respect that. I know your eyes are open to what he's done and who he is, and if you trust him, then I should trust him too."

"Should?" I repeated.

"I'm working on it," he said. "But right now I really do need to go."

"We haven't talked to Loke yet," I said.

"*That* conversation would likely go better without me there," he said. He turned towards the front door and I trailed along behind him.

"That's likely true," I admitted. "But this Báfurr fellow?" He stopped in the middle of buttoning up his heavy wool coat.

"I should be there for that conversation," he said. "But I don't know when I'll be free." He resumed buttoning his coat up to his neck, but I could see the gears in his mind were still turning. "If you need to speak to him before I'm back, take Loke with you. And Roarr. Yes, take both."

"It would be like that time I went to talk to Raggi in Aldís' mead hall, wouldn't it?" I guessed. "Don't these guys ever go home where I can talk to them one on one?"

"If you make it an official action of the council, my brothers and I could summon him there to be questioned," he said.

"Is that a good idea?"

"I don't know," he admitted. "Those types already don't like you because of where you grew up. But they don't particularly like the council either. Too friendly with outsiders for their tastes."

"I thought that was just my grandmother they didn't like," I said.

"We trade a lot with the outside world, and they don't approve," Thorbjorn said. "I mean, just what we've had this morning, coffee and cinnamon don't grow here."

"The council lets that stuff in?" I asked. He nodded. "And they, these isolationists as Roarr called them, don't like it?"

"It's all or nothing with them," he said. "They're a tough sort. Difficult to deal with. But the last time we had trolls roaming too close to town, they were indispensable. It's worth tolerating their extreme views."

"Is it?" I asked.

"You're new here," he reminded me.

"You're right," I said. "I have a lot to learn, a lot to see and absorb. But at the end of all that, I don't think I'm going to be any more okay with extremists telling me I don't belong."

"Of course not," he said with a little smile. "I'll see you as soon as I can."

"Yeah," I said. "Stay safe. If you're doing anything dangerous. Which you probably are."

His little smile grew into a wide grin, but then he was gone.

I was still standing in my front hall trying to figure out what to do next when a knock on the door startled me out of my thoughts. I opened the door to see Nilda and Kara.

"Thorbjorn left?" Kara asked, looking back over her shoulder.

"We saw him on the street," Nilda said with a conspiratorial gleam to her eye.

"Yeah, he had a thing. Do you guys want to come in?" I asked.

"We come bearing a message from Loke," Nilda said, extending a folded sheet of paper towards me. I stepped back out of the way to look at the note while the sisters got out of their coats and boots.

"He can't come up here? Really?" I said, scanning over the note's few lines a second time.

"He's not faking," Nilda said, her face grave. "He's been sneaking out at night, but during the day he's been at his sister's side constantly."

"Is she sick?" I asked, turning the note over as if there might be some writing on the other side that I had missed. There wasn't.

"She's on the mend for now," Kara said. "I think he might be exercising an abundance of caution, not leaving her alone."

"But sneaking out at night is okay?" I asked. "What if she takes a turn while he's gone?"

Kara shrugged. "Do you know how to get there?" she asked.

"More or less," I said. "He's pointed it out to me from here. It's down in the valley surrounded by trees."

"Just follow the south road past the cow pastures until you get to the huge ramshackle house that looks like a stiff wind would blow it over," Nilda said. "Kara and I will stay here and answer the door for you. Did Roarr get here already? We went to his place first, and we'd clearly woken him up."

"Yes, he was here," I said. "Thanks."

"I suppose it's too soon to know who did it?" Kara asked.

"Definitely too soon," I said. "And I'm not sure Loke will be much help. But he did help Sigvin get Nefja home last night. Perhaps he saw something that Sigvin didn't."

I zipped up my parka and snugged my wool hat low over my eyes before pulling on my mittens. Even with all that, the first breath of air that entered my lungs when I stepped outside burned. It was like I could feel the air sacs in my lungs shriveling up to escape that cold.

My boots crunched over snow and ice as I opened then closed my garden gate and turned to follow the road due south.

And saw Mjolner sitting quietly in the middle of the road as if waiting for me. As usual, the cold seemed to bother him not at all. That *had* to be weird for a cat. He turned and led the way down the road, and I followed, thrusting my mittened hands into my parka pockets.

Whatever my cat thought, it was really cold.

We reached the public gardens, but Mjolner kept on going, leaving the end of the road behind to follow one of the garden paths past the greenhouses. Then the cobblestoned path became a track through the snow. The roads in town were all carefully shoveled clear of snow, but this path was little more than a pair of vehicle wheel tracks in the snow, mostly obliterated by bootprints.

Mjolner walked lightly over the top of the snow, but I kept breaking through the crusty upper layer to the softer, wetter lower layers that clung to my boots. It was slow going.

But aside from the aching cold, it was actually a really lovely day for a walk. The sun was raising ever higher in a bright blue sky, reflecting off the snow on the ground and the frost on the trees like someone had covered the world in glitter.

I knew the fields around me were for dairy cows, but at first they seemed empty. It was only when I reached the bottom of that largest hill that I reached the first of the farmhouses. Then I saw the cows, clustered close to their barns in warmth-conserving huddles close to their feeding troughs.

I could hardly blame them. But they didn't look particularly miserable, just mildly curious, chewing their cud as they watched me trudge by.

Then the road crossed another road at a sharp angle. Now I was facing two roads that were both heading more or less directly south. If it weren't for Mjolner following the left-hand road as if the other didn't even exist to him, I don't know what I would've done. Wandered around for hours in the cold, maybe.

We crossed a few more hills, more low and rolling than the one that Villmark stood atop of, with its semi-panoramic view of Lake Superior. Here there was no sign of the lake, just snow-covered hill after snow-covered hill, dotted with the occasional cows.

Then Mjolner took another turn, up a path of sparse bootprints but no sign of wagon wheels on the snow. We were heading due west now, into a sort of hollow nestled between two taller ranges of hills. And before us was a house, a very Gothic-looking house by Minnesotan standards, let alone the more minimalist/modernist look favored by the people of Villmark. Tall trees flanked it on all sides, overshadowing it even now when they had no leaves to speak of.

It looked even more lonely and remote than it had from my great room window.

And yet on either side of that narrow path were hills covered with the fattest cows I had seen yet. But the fences all led away from this place, not towards it. Those cows belonged to someone else.

One of the cows made a moo sound, and I looked to see it standing right at the edge of the fence, watching me with big brown eyes. It had a little white patch, maybe paler hair or maybe a scar where hair couldn't grow, right above its eye.

And it was in the shape of Fe.

I blinked hard, but when I looked again, it was still there. Then I looked past it at a group of three cows a little distance away. They all had Fe marks on them as well. Every cow I looked at, the same thing.

Well, Haraldr had warned me about this. I just hadn't expected it to be so obvious. Cows were not the deeper meaning of Fe, after all, but the most direct one.

Mjolner was waiting for me at the front door, and I climbed the steps up onto the porch and raised a hand to knock.

But my hand hovered there, unmoving, as my eyes picked out a pattern in the wood of the door. Was that Fe upside-down?

I gave myself a little shake. After not seeing anything all day yesterday despite my many efforts, it was a little annoying I couldn't stop seeing things now. The house I was standing in frcnt of was the very definition of something that had once been a sign of wealth but was now falling into worthlessness. I didn't need magic senses to perceive that.

I took a deep cleansing breath and then knocked on the door.

CHAPTER THIRTEEN

I was expecting to have to knock more than once. Loke was expecting me, but the house was immense by Villmark standards. Without a doorbell, I wasn't sure if my mittened hand could knock loud enough to carry throughout that place.

But I heard the sound of a bolt sliding open, and then the door itself swung inwards. At first I couldn't see anything but gloom within and felt a twinge of trepidation in my stomach.

Then I would swear Mjolner gave me a look of exasperation before plunging into the house, tail up high, the top of it gently curving back and forth like a question mark and then a backward question mark.

"Ingrid," Loke said, and stepped forward from the blackness to a grayness that at least let me make out his roughest features.

"I got your note," I said. "Is everything all right?"

"Perfectly," he said. "I'm sorry about the darkness. Light is one of the things that triggers Esja's headaches. But your eyes will adjust once you're inside."

"Oh," I said, realizing he was waving his arm to hurry me in. I didn't see his sister anywhere inside, but I couldn't see much, and at any rate I knew how blinding the full sun was on the fields of snow. I hustled inside, and Loke shut the door behind me.

At first I saw nothing but the explosions of light against my retinas that were the aftereffects of that last look back at the snow. But slowly I started to see that I was standing in a front hall of a house nothing like any of the other homes in Villmark. This was more like an old English manor with two curving staircases before me, a marble floor patterned like a checkerboard below me, and open double doors to either side leading into further, even darker rooms.

"There's a coat rack behind you," Loke said as I untied my boots to leave them on the mat by the door. I say mat, but this wasn't the size of your standard doormat. It was more like a flying carpet. But it was clearly designed to deal with wet things. I turned to see the ornate wooden coat rack behind me, holding a single black coat that I recognized as Loke's. I hung my own beside it, hat and mittens stuffed in the pockets.

"It's just the two of you here?" I asked.

"Yes, currently," Loke said. "I'm sure you have a lot of questions, but let me give you what's probably going to be the most frequent answer up front. I don't know. I don't know why this place looks like it does, like it belongs neither to Old Norway nor to northern Minnesota. I don't know which of my ancestors even built the place. I don't know why it's so large. I've traced back my family tree, and no one in it ever had enough kids to fill a place like this."

"Does it bother you? All that mystery?" I asked. It would drive me crazy. I could never live with so many "I don't know" answers. I'd have to find out more.

But Loke just shrugged. "I've always lived here. It's not so strange to me. Of course, the place nearly burned down when I was a child." He waved for me to follow him into one of the side rooms, a sort of parlor with chairs gathered around an ornate marble fireplace. But he rushed through it to get to the far side, turning a key in a lock to open a second set of double doors.

I could smell the smoke from within even before I reached his side to look into the fire-damaged room beyond. It was an old smoke smell, and from what Loke had told me I'd guess it was smoke from two decades ago or more, but it lingered all the same. I could see where the fire had started at the corner fireplace, scorching the walls and charring the timbers that supported the ceiling.

"You've never gotten it fixed?" I asked.

He shrugged again. "It's easier just to lock the door, and the door to the room above it."

"That was your parents' room?" I said.

He looked over at me. I could see sadness in his eyes, but also I could see that he was impressed by my guess.

"Yes. Have you eaten?" he asked in a brighter tone.

"I had a cinnamon roll. Sort of," I said. I could remember taking a bite, but I was pretty sure most of it was still on a plate on my kitchen table back at home.

"I was about to call Esja down for breakfast," he said. "Nothing fancy, just porridge. She keeps to a bland diet. But there's honey and fruit and nuts for the rest of us."

"That sounds really good, actually," I said. "It was a pretty cold walk. Nothing like having a little something warm to eat to chase the cold out."

I followed Loke back out to the main hall and then towards the back of the house, through a pair of doors that had been hiding in the shadows between the staircases. We crossed a formal dining room with a table long enough to seat a dozen people, more if they were cozy. Sideboards waited on either end of the table to hold a buffet of dishes, and the chairs all had tall backs, the better to close in the space around the diners as they chatted and ate together.

But the chandelier over the table was thick with dust, and the table had a dull sheen to it, as if its wood surface hadn't been polished in... well, decades.

The far end of the room led into the kitchen. This at least felt cozy. The only light was from the open door of a wood-burning stove that sat in the center of the room, but at least it was a cheery light, not the gray through the dirty windows I had grown accustomed to. It was a large kitchen, clearly designed to let a crew of cooks work together to load up that massive table in the other room, but I could tell that Loke and his sister favored the space closest to that stove. There was a little table there, two matching chairs at either end with a third mismatched chair pulled up, I was sure, just for me.

But there was also a young woman there, setting bowls down on the table. She was wearing a long white dress that looked like a nightgown, soft and comfortable, but warmer than any nightgown I had ever owned. Her long blond hair was pulled back from her face by a white ribbon, then left to tumble down her back. It had only been haphazardly brushed; I could see the remains of tangles I imagined had been deemed too stubborn and left alone.

She looked up as we came into the room and smiled, just a soft curve to her lips, no wider. Nothing like her brother's exuberant smiles.

"Esja," Loke said, rushing to take the bowls from her. But she lunged for the table, setting them down before he could stop her.

"I'm not completely useless, you know," she said.

"I know," he said. "But this is not one of your uses, surely."

"As much as I would love to hear a full list of my many uses, we have company, brother," she said pointedly.

"Oh, yes. Are introductions really in order? No one is confused about who they're looking at, surely," he said.

"I'm Ingrid," I said, leaning forward to extend my hand to Esja. "Pleased to meet you."

"Esja, and likewise," she said, putting her hand in mine. It was cold and thin and I worried I might squeeze it too hard, but she had no compunction about squeezing mine. She was stronger than she looked.

"Porridge, then?" Loke said, heading towards the cookstove.

"I made tea as well," Esja said, crossing the room to fetch a pot wrapped in a tea towel from one of the prep tables. I sat down in the mismatched chair, the better to stay out of their way.

Soon we were all gathered together, and I had laden my bowl of porridge with blueberries, honey, slivers of almonds, and a sprinkle of brown sugar before pouring a little dollop of cream over it. It was like dessert for breakfast, really, but I needed the fuel. I ate a spoonful and followed it up by a sip of the surprisingly strong tea, and felt the warmth hit my stomach and then spread throughout my body.

"So, Loke," I started to say, but he caught my eye and gave a little shake of his head. He wasn't ready to talk yet. Fine. I could wait until after breakfast, or brunch, or whatever.

"Loke tells me that you're an artist," Esja said, her eyes bright.

"I am," I admitted, curious why he had said artist and not volva.

"Esja also likes to sketch," he said, as if reading my mind. "She even paints watercolors these days."

"I've just started trying that," Esja said, her cheeks flushing pink. "I don't quite have the hang of it yet. Mostly it feels like a good way to ruin a perfectly adequate sketch."

"Daily practice is usually the best remedy," I said. "I don't have time today, but I'd love to sit with you sometime and watch you work. I don't do much watercolor myself, but I did have a class in it at art school."

"Ooh, you've been to *art school,*" she said, crushing her napkin in her hands and pressing it to her chin in perfect rapture.

"Yes, before I moved here," I said.

"I would love to go to school," she said wistfully.

"Art school?" I asked.

"Any kind of school," she said. "Business school, that sounds interesting. Or something technical like structural engineering."

"Structural engineering?" I repeated, a bit dumbfounded. Her list seemed a little random.

"I bring Esja books from the racks your grandmother has in the general store in Runde," Loke told me. I had completely forgotten that during the day, when it wasn't a mead hall, the Runde meeting hall was also a general store as well as a post office. And my grandmother ran it all.

And apparently that general store still sold paperbacks in spinning wire racks.

"I liked those books well enough, but now that there's an actual bookstore, Loke has been bringing me proper books," Esja said with great enthusiasm.

"Romance novels," Loke told me. "She liked the little dime store ones well enough, but Jessica has more modern ones."

"And the women have such interesting jobs!" Esja said.

"Like business management and structural engineering," I guessed.

"Yes! They live such interesting lives," she said with a happy sigh.

"Don't scarcely need the men to have adventures, do they?" Loke said, but low so that only I heard him. I smothered a grin. There was a certain irony, considering that Esja in this half-burned shambles of an ancestral home, was only missing a few more mysterious elements like a ghost in the attic or something evil in the basement to be living the exact sort of Gothic tale all those business women and structural engineers were reading in their spare time.

"Have you never been down to Runde yourself?" I asked. "Surely Loke would take you if you asked."

"He would," Esja said. "He would if I asked."

A pallor fell over the three of us. I had clearly asked the wrong thing and steered the whole conversation to a dark place. I wanted to bring us back to something lighter, but I wasn't sure what topic would do it.

"I would carry her there, if she asked me to," Loke said, but Esja put up a hand, begging him to stop.

"Are you all right?" I asked. It was hard to tell in the soft lightening, but she seemed to be getting paler, or grayer.

"I'll be all right," she said, but she looked slumped in her chair, like a stuffed animal that had been propped up for a tea party.

"It's been a lot of excitement," Loke said. "Do you need-"

But she put up her hand again, and he broke off at once. "I'll be all right. Please, stay with our guest. I know you have things to discuss. I know this get together wasn't about me."

"I wanted you two to meet," Loke said, half getting out of his chair as she put both hands on the table to leverage herself up to her feet.

"I'll be fine," she said. "I'm just going to lie down."

"Upstairs?" he asked.

"No. I'll be in the back parlor," she said. Then she looked up at me. "Ingrid, it was so very good to meet you. I hope I'll see you again soon, on a better day."

"I hope so too," I said. She smiled, then made her way across the room. She reached out for the back of this chair, or the edge of that table, before reaching the support of the doorway. She stopped for a moment as if to gather herself before continuing on. Then she was out of sight.

"Loke," I started to say.

"Not yet," he said. "I just need a minute." He was staring fixedly at his half-eaten porridge. But then in a burst of energy he started gathering up the breakfast dishes and carrying them to the sink.

"There's something you're not telling me," I said.

He scoffed. "There are lots of things I don't tell you, Ingy," he said. But his back was to me as he stood at the sink and I couldn't see his face.

"What's wrong with your sister?" I asked.

"Nothing that needs to concern you," he said. "Please, just give me a minute. Just one minute and then I'll answer every question you have about last night."

"All right," I agreed.

For the moment. The time would come when he'd have to open up to me about the rest of it. But for now, my focus was on Nefja and finding her killer. The rest would have to wait.

CHAPTER FOURTEEN

WHILE LOKE FINISHED his washing up, I got up from the table to wander around the kitchen. I looked at the rack of cast-iron cookware hanging over one of the prep tables and saw an inverted Fe in the oily sheen of many of the pots and pans. I looked down at the table itself and saw it again, flashing out at me from the woodwork.

It was there again, traced in the dust caked to one window like a child had traced it with a fingertip. It was in the paneling. It was worked into the pattern of the marble floor.

I stopped looking around, tilting my head back to press the heels of my hands into my eyes. I was probably just too tired. And too suggestible, just like Haraldr had said.

Perhaps after I talked with Loke, I should call on Haraldr. Now that I had something to tell him other than about my long day and night of failure.

"Ingrid?" Loke asked. I took my hands off my eyes to see him looking at me questioningly as he dried his hands on a towel.

"Just tired," I said. He gave me a skeptical look, but I ignored it. "Where's my cat? He came in here with me."

"Probably with Esja," Loke said with a careless shrug. "He comes here all the time, you know."

"Of course he does," I said. He had a more active social life than I did, that was for sure. "Ready to talk?"

"Let's go outside," he said.

"What about your sister?" I asked.

"She's resting," he said, glancing back towards the doorway she had disappeared through. "I'm not leaving. We'll just walk up to the road. That should be enough time to cover everything I can tell you."

"That doesn't sound like enough," I said, but he was already heading back through the dining room. I followed him. We both bundled up and headed back out into the cold, dry air.

"How much of this property is yours?" I asked as we crunched over the snow.

"None of it now except the house," he said. "But when this place was built, everything you could see all around here was my family's. They didn't sell it off all at once, but bit by bit it dwindled away. I suppose the cows you see now are descendants of my family's cows, once upon a time. But they aren't ours now."

"Do you go into town every night?" I asked.

"You know I don't," he said.

"Half the time in Runde?" I guessed.

"Not even," he said. "Look, I wouldn't go out at all, except sometimes I just feel a pull. You know what I mean." He gave me a sidelong look.

"I'm not sure I do," I said. "Are you talking about magic?"

He shrugged. "I don't label things. But sometimes, after Esja goes to bed, I just feel like there's a place I have to be. So I leave the house, and wherever I end up, I guess that must've been the place."

"Because you do something important?"

"Who knows?" he said. "Maybe sometimes. I doubt all the time I'm really *all* that needed. But I go out all the same. Maybe I'm just pretending there's a call because I need to get out."

"I don't think so," I said. "I think if you wanted to go out, you'd just say so. I don't think Esja would mind."

"You've just met Esja," he said, giving me another sneaking glance. "Do you think she'd object to anything I did?"

"No," I admitted.

"So clearly she can't be the guideline for my behavior."

"Is there someone else you feel you answer to?" I asked.

He gave a little irritated shake of his head. "We've gotten off track. You were meant to be asking me about last night. I went to the mead hall, as you know. I got there after the party was in full swing, Nefja even more so. I could see that Roarr was feeling particularly trapped. So I helped him out." He lifted his hands as if to say end of story, but there was no way I was letting it go with that.

"It was more than that," I said. "First of all, the mere presence of Sigvin is generally enough for you to flee any scene, and yet this time you intervened on Roarr's behalf knowing full well she was right there and you couldn't avoid her."

"You exaggerate," he said.

"Do I?" I asked skeptically. "Does Roarr need your protection? Because you came to his aid the other night when I was there, if you recall."

"I remember perfectly well," Loke said. "I do what amuses me. I don't care to ascribe motives to all of it, not in the moment, and certainly not after the fact."

"I would swear you don't want to confront the fact that you might be a nice guy," I said. "A good friend."

"Stop it," he said. His tone was joking, but I knew he was serious.

"You helped Sigvin get Nefja home," I said. "Nefja so far gone by that point that you were essentially putting yourself in a position to be alone with Sigvin."

"That's not as big of a thing as you seem to think," he said.

"She invited you to stay," I said.

He raised his eyebrows. "She told you that? But it doesn't matter. It was just an offer to crash on her parents' spare bed, and I turned it down. That's all."

"Where did you go afterwards?" I asked.

"I walked home," he said.

"Directly?" I asked.

He grabbed my elbow to drag me to a halt and turned to face me. "Ingrid, am I a suspect?"

"Should you be?" I countered.

"No," he said.

"Did you see anything on your walk home?" I asked. "Did you hear anything while you were out on the streets?"

"No," he said. "Nothing at all. I was home and asleep straight afterwards, and didn't know anything had gone amiss until Nilda and Kara woke me up pounding on my door this morning."

"There are only so many streets in Villmark," I said. "You were out walking them. Roarr was out walking them too. Neither of you saw each other, or Nefja, who must have left her parents' house at some point, or the person who I heard running away. Can you explain that?"

"You honestly think if I need a walk to clear my head that I only walk these streets? In this town? In this world?"

"You went north? Into the forest?" I asked.

He shook his head, giving me an irritated look. "I can walk in more worlds than you know, and when I'm in them, I never see the likes of Roarr wandering around with me." He looked away, pressing his fingers to the bridge of his nose.

He was wincing.

"Are you all right?" I asked.

"Fine," he snapped, which wasn't like him. I pulled back from him, just a bit, but he noticed. "I'm fine, Ingrid," he said more softly. "My sister isn't the only person in this world who's entitled to a headache from time to time."

"Maybe there's something wrong with your house," I said, looking back over my shoulder at the sorry-looking building. "The fire damage still smells like smoke; that can't be good. Or it could be black mold. Or radon gas even."

"It's not black mold or radon," he said. At first he sounded thoroughly world weary, but then he straightened his shoulders and gave me a look with just a touch of something merry back in his eyes. "Trust you to start with the mundane."

"Have you had it checked?" I asked. "We can get test kits. Maybe not in Runde, but I can mail order things for you."

"It's all right, Ingrid," he said. "My house is not your problem."

"So you're saying it *is* a problem?" I asked.

He laughed but shook his head. "Look, I have to get back. Did you have any other questions?"

I stomped my feet as I mulled it over. It was far too cold for standing about. "Báfurr," I said at last.

"What about him?" Loke asked with a frown.

"You saw he was there," I said.

"With some of his friends," he said. "They were behaving. Keeping to themselves."

"Báfurr approached Nefja at least twice and was rejected," I said.

"I didn't see any of that," Loke said with a shrug. "But he's a stoic type. He doesn't really have a temper to speak of. Not that I particularly like the guy, but that's my honest assessment. If she had pushed him to anger, we would've seen it there in the mead hall. It wouldn't have been something he nursed to act out on later."

"So you know him well?" I asked.

He shrugged again. "As well as anybody."

I frowned. That just wasn't good enough for me. But I had never met the man. I had no idea what my gut would be telling me if I did. Maybe it would agree with Loke.

"I should probably go talk to him next," I said.

"Sure. Maybe not alone, though," Loke said.

I frowned at him. "Thorbjorn said the same thing. And yet you just said he didn't have a temper."

"His thing with outsiders isn't really a blistering rage thing," he said. "It's more a part of his very soul. I'm not saying he would hurt you. I don't think he would. But if you really need to get answers out of him, bring someone with that he'll talk to. But not me. I've got to get back to Esja."

"How she was today, is that better or worse than usual?" I asked.

He thought it over. "Middling," he said at last. Then he turned to go, but before he was out of earshot he turned to shout over his shoulder. "Take a Thor with you to talk to Báfurr. Or at least a Roarr."

"I will," I said, but he just trudged away from me over the icy snow.

CHAPTER FIFTEEN

IT WAS NEARLY lunchtime by the time I came back in my front door, so it was scarcely surprising to find Nilda and Kara in my kitchen making sandwiches.

The amount of sandwiches *was* a surprise. They were covering my largest serving platter with a towering pyramid of them. And these weren't dainty finger sandwiches, either. These were thick slices of meat and cheese between equally thick slices of dark rye bread.

"Why are you feeding an army?" I asked from the kitchen doorway, and they both jumped.

"It's not quite enough for an army," Nilda said defensively.

"Are you really that hungry?" I asked.

"You have guests," Kara said as she picked up the platter and swept past me to bring it out to my great room.

"Guests?" I asked Nilda.

"Thorbjorn and Thorge are here," Nilda said. "They brought Báfurr, who in turn brought three of his friends. Roarr is here as well; I'm not sure why. But the mood in that room is more than a little tense. I thought a bit of food might help keep that animosity on a low simmer."

"Good thinking," I said.

"Did you learn anything useful at Loke's house?" Thorbjorn asked as he came into the kitchen. He had a sandwich in each hand and took a bite from one and chewed as he waited for me to answer.

"Not particularly," I said. "I think he arrived at the mead hall too late and left too soon to really learn much. You certainly got back her fast for someone who was acting like he'd be gone for days just a couple of hours ago."

"I had to rearrange some things with my brothers," he said. "We're stretched a little thin, but hopefully this case won't take long to solve. But Thorge felt personally involved since he was the one that brought her up out of the well. So the other three are standing watch at the bonfire and patrolling the hills to cover for the two of us. Thorge and I are entirely at your disposal."

"And the first thing you did was bring Báfurr in," I said. "That's handy. He was the next person I needed to talk to. Maybe the last person, since I haven't uncovered anything like a lead."

"Yes, I knew he'd be on the top of your list," he said. He shoved the last of the first sandwich into his mouth and I had to wait for him to chew and swallow it down before he went on. "I'm glad you listened to me and waited for me to question him. When Thorge and I found him at Aldís' mead hall, he was already in a prickly mood."

"Why?" I asked.

"He knows he's a suspect," Thorbjorn said. "Or at least he thinks that's why you want to talk to him. Rumors have been spreading, and I think some of those friends of his have told him he's likely to take the blame regardless of his guilt or innocence."

"That's not how I work," I said.

"I know that," he said. "He's determined to assume all sorts of things about you because you're from the outside world. I'm here to help you balance that out."

"Thanks for that," I said.

"Sandwich?" he asked, offering me his uneaten one.

"No, thanks," I said. "I just ate like an hour ago, and that looks like I'd need a nap straightaway after eating it."

Thorbjorn looked down at the sandwich, then shrugged and took a large bite out of it.

"I think we might need a few more," Kara said as she came back into the kitchen with the now-empty platter. Then she saw Thorbjorn with a sandwich still in his hand. "Oh, hi there, Thorbjorn. Do you like the sandwiches? Nilda and I brought smoked elk from home. It's the last of last winter's hunt, but it was such tasty meat. I don't know what that elk had been grazing on, but it definitely wasn't the usual stuff. And we make that cheese ourselves too."

Thorbjorn hurriedly swallowed, then gave her a smile.

I swear I could see melt her knees from across the room.

"It's very good, Kara," he said, and she gripped the back of one of my kitchen chairs to keep from swooning to the floor. He went on eating, oblivious.

"The food is working," Thorge said as he came into the kitchen as well. Nilda was on her way out with another plate of food and motioned for him to clear the doorway. He stumbled up against Kara still gripping that chair back, putting a hand on her shoulder to keep from bowling her over.

Then very reluctantly removing his hand. He swept his hands over his hair, cut practically in a mohawk to show off the tattoos that arced over both of his ears. I could see him trying to find something to say to Kara.

"Nilda said something about apples?" he said. "Apples with some of that particularly sharp cheese you make would be perfection, I should think. You make such good cheese."

"Nilda just took them out," Kara said, only sparing him half a glance before turning back to smile up at Thorbjorn.

I stepped back to lean against my kitchen counter and pressed a hand to my forehead. Partly I was trying to hide the smile that kept threatening to break out over my face, but partly I was also just really tired. Which maybe was why my emotional responses were running away from me.

Still, there was a certain irony in it all. I was trying to solve a mystery that involved so many interlocking circles of unrequited interest, and now there were even more on display here in my own kitchen.

Then the memory of my last moment of Andrew washed over me, so vivid it was like I could feel my hand gripping the sleeve of his parka, smell the cold snow that had been all around us. I was immersed again in that silvery world of the nearly full moon reflecting off a world of ice.

"Ingrid?" Thorbjorn said, and I dropped my hand.

"Yes?" I said. But there was a hint of worry in his eyes, so I added, "I'm fine. Just... thinking."

"About?" he prompted.

"Well, apparently there's quite a crowd in my great room just now, but that's not how I want to conduct this interview."

"Agreed," he said. "Thorge, go back out there and let Báfurr know we'll be calling him in in a minute. And he's to come in here without his friends. They can wait for him out there."

"He's going to be grumpy about that," Thorge sighed. Then he looked down at Kara. "Maybe you can help me convince him?"

"Me?" she said.

"You have a way about you. I bet you could get him to do anything just by asking," he said.

"That's not been *my* experience with men," Kara said with a frown. But then she shrugged. "Well, it can't hurt to try. I think Ingrid and Thorbjorn are trying to kick us out, anyway." Her tone was joking, but her eyes were just a little hurt.

"We only need a minute to compare notes," I said, perhaps too quickly.

"We'll call for Báfurr when we're ready, and he comes in alone," Thorbjorn said to his brother.

Thorge nodded, drawing up tall and just barely touching his hands to the hilts of his sword and axe.

Then he and Kara were gone.

"He likes her," Thorbjorn said, leaning in close and whispering as if telling me some delightful secret.

"I noticed that," I said. I waited for him to go on, to mention the other part I'd noticed about Kara and her feelings, but he just looked pleased with that little bit he'd told me. I sighed, then decided to drop the matter. "Like I said, I didn't really learn anything from Loke. He didn't see anything suspicious, and Nefja was quite out of it when he left her and Sigvin. He says he went home after but didn't see anything of importance."

"Do you think she got up and left the house on her own for some reason?" Thorbjorn asked. "It doesn't seem likely, but the idea that someone went into her house to bring her out of it is just chilling."

"I don't know," I admitted. "Unless Báfurr's story gives us anything more to go on, I might have to turn to magic after this. Everything else has been a dead end."

"You're still sure this is a murder and not a terrible accident?" he asked.

"Logically, I'd have to say I can't be sure of any such thing," I admitted.

"But?" he prompted.

"But my bones tell me it was a murder," I said.

"I trust your bones," he said. "I know you can't go down the hill to speak with your grandmother, but if you need her, I can go fetch her for you."

"Thank you for the offer," I said. "I don't think I need to take you up on that just yet. I still have things to try."

I didn't add that it had only been a day since I'd seen her last. If I couldn't make it through a day on my own, how was I going to make it through the entire probation period the council had sentenced me to?

"Are we ready for our witness, then?" he asked.

"Yes," I said. "Let's get on with it."

As he went out towards the great room, I settled into what was already becoming my personal chair at the kitchen table. I took a deep breath and prepared myself to hear the same story all over again from yet a different point of view.

CHAPTER SIXTEEN

THORBJORN CAME BACK into the kitchen and gave me a look that was something between a warning and a preemptive apology. I raised my own eyebrows to ask for clarification, but he just shook his head.

Then a second man came in behind him, his face a dark scowl, his gait an aggressive march entirely out of place in my cozy little kitchen.

I didn't exactly know what it meant legally when lawyers on TV asked the judge for permission to treat the witness as hostile. But I really wished there was a judge there now for me to ask that of.

He was very, very hostile. And I hadn't even asked him any questions yet.

"I'm only here because I want justice for Nefja," he said as he slammed his way down into the seat across from me. He spit the words out in rapid Villmarker Norse, his accent so thick I was sure he was putting it on. Which seemed strange, since I was sure his emotions were real.

"That's why we're all here," Thorbjorn said in English as he slid into the seat between us.

Báfurr sneered but said nothing.

"You're skeptical?" I asked, also in English.

He glared at me and I held his gaze steadily, my hands calmly folded on the table in front of me. Inside I was quaking, but I didn't let it show. I just waited.

Finally, he shifted in his chair and looked away from me. "I won't speak your tongue," he said.

"Fine," I said in careful Villmarker Norse. "I can follow you well enough. And if I have trouble, Thorbjorn is here to assist me. So don't feel like you have to choose simple words or speak slowly on my account. We can handle whatever you have to say however you wish to say it. The important thing is that you tell us everything."

He scowled again, but it was more annoyance than anger this time.

"Do you understand?" Thorbjorn asked in Villmarker Norse.

"Yes," Báfurr snapped. "You must already know what happened last night."

"We want to hear your side of it from you," I said. "You came in with some friends. Are they the same friends in the other room now?"

"No," Báfurr said. "I'm the only one you'll be talking to about this."

Thorbjorn started to scowl at him, but I quickly said, "fine."

"Fine," Thorbjorn agreed with obvious reluctance. "Tell us your story from when you came in."

"I was there with friends to eat dinner and drink ale, to enjoy the warmth and light of a fire on a cold, dark night," Báfurr said.

"But it's not your usual choice of mead hall," I said.

"No, as you well know," he said. "And as I'm sure you also well know, we were there because I wanted to see Nefja."

"Yes," I said.

"Well, she was there," he said brusquely. But then he took a deeper breath and I could see he was imagining the scene in more detail, searching his memory to get everything exactly right. "Sigvin and Nefja were drinking a mug of ale together, the remains of their meal still before them. Four plates, but it was just the two of them when we came in." His eyes were half-closed, and he raised a hand to point off to his right. "Roarr was near the kitchens, one of the serving girls already hanging off of him."

"Hanging off of him?" I asked. "Physically?"

He gave me a withering look. "You know what I mean."

"I don't," I said. "This is a new wrinkle in this story. Was she on his lap or what?"

"No," he said. "But while the rest of us waited to be served, Roarr got plate after plate of things he hadn't even ordered. His cup was always full while my friends and I waved several times before getting her attention each time our own mugs were dry."

"She isn't the only woman who works there,' Thorbjorn said.

"The others have to hustle to make up the difference," Báfurr said. "Have you interviewed the staff yet?"

"Not yet," Thorbjorn said.

"Sigvin and Nefja were drinking," I said, trying to bring the story back on track.

"Yes, and Nefja was getting wild," he said.

"Drunk?" I asked.

He twisted his mouth up as he made a judgment. "Not yet. But she was flushed, and she was fired up. Very angry. She was declaring to everyone in the hall around her that she was done waiting around for Roarr. Either he crossed that room and took her hand, or she was moving on."

"So you approached her?" Thorbjorn asked.

"It seemed the opportune time," he said, but his tone was sarcastic, like he was seeing the irony now that he hadn't then.

"You'd talked to her before," I said.

"Of course I'd talked to her before," he sneered at me.

"No, I mean, you'd proposed to her before," I said.

"Twice before," he said. "She turned me down both times, but there was alway something in her eyes like regret. I knew she was hung up on Roarr. She had been since we were kids. First that outsider woman was in her way, and I felt her pain at that. To come second to someone so unworthy. But she didn't want my shoulder to cry on. And now, even when he was single, he wouldn't have her. Who is he to turn down such a creature?"

"Lisa is too newly dead for him," I said, but he scoffed at that.

"What did you say to Nefja?" Thorbjorn asked.

"Nothing inappropriate, I assure you," Báfurr said. "She is a woman of Villmark, and I treated her as such."

"So you said?" Thorbjorn prompted.

"I told her again of my farm to the west of the village, and of my many goats and sheep, of my skill with fishing as well as with hunting. With me as a husband, she'd never have a reason to worry about anything ever again. She wouldn't have to rely on things from that outside world. I could provide everything she would ever need. I would care for her like the precious treasure she was."

I bit my tongue to hold back the incredulous words, "and that didn't work?" to say instead, "she said no?"

"She said no," Báfurr said.

"Still with that regret in her eyes?" Thorbjorn asked, with not even a hint of a joking tone.

"Her words were harsh and direct," Báfurr conceded, looking down at the tabletop and not at either of us. "But yes, I still saw something there." Then he buried his face in his hands so suddenly I nearly jumped in my seat. "Do you know what it's like? I love her. *Loved* her," he amended, his voice catching. "But before she would have me, that cretin would have to get it over with and break her heart. And she'd be destroyed, and it would kill me to see it, to see her that way. Heartbroken for someone so unworthy of her. To have such a step be necessary before we had our happiness, it kills me."

"You've given this some thought," Thorbjorn said neutrally.

Báfurr dropped his hands and glared at him, his eyes glassy but not wet with tears. "Of course I have. What else is there to do during the long sleepless nights?"

"What happened next?" I asked.

Báfurr shrugged. "I went back to my friends and had another mug of ale. I knew I'd have to wait and try again later. But I knew eventually she'd wear down. Eventually she'd say yes. So I felt no anger even though, as I've said, her words last night were particularly harsh."

"And she went over to Roarr," I said.

"Yes, she did," he said. His finger was tracing over and over a crack in the woodwork of my table as if it were a scratch he could buff out. "Did you want me to guess whether I had spurred her to do that?"

"No, no conjecture necessary," Thorbjorn said.

"So Nefja was all over Roarr, and I was pleased to see it, actually," Báfurr said, but his tone didn't quite convince me that was true. "At last this was the moment. She was going to push him too far, and he was going to break her heart for good and all. And I think Roarr was about to snap. I could see it. Even that shell of a man was going to manage to find his backbone at last in another handful of minutes.

"But then Loke came in, and everything changed. He distracted Nefja long enough for Roarr to escape out the back," he said those last four words with rising contempt, then shook his head with a humorless laugh. "And Sigvin wanted to thank Loke because of course she did, and Nefja was alone and for once she looked like she might be just a little bit broken."

Thorbjorn bristled at this description, but I put a hand on his and signaled for him to let Báfurr keep talking.

"But I was wrong. The wound was too raw, perhaps. Certainly she had had too much ale. I should've seen that. Better to wait until morning when she would remember our conversation with more clarity. But, alas, I was afraid if I missed that moment that another would never come." He barked out another dry laugh. "And I was right, wasn't I?"

"She turned you down again," I said softly.

"More cruelly than before," he said, his finger rubbing at that crack in the table again. "But I forgave it. Even as she was still speaking the words, I forgave her. Who doesn't say things they don't mean after so many mugs of ale? After being so publicly rejected, having been made a fool of by that meddler Loke, still I had no bad feelings in my heart for her. I forgave her at once, and I forgive her still."

"Loke and Sigvin took her home then?" I guessed.

"Yes," he said.

"And you went home as well?" I asked.

"No," he said and stopped rubbing the crack to look up at me. "I was in Aldís' mead hall after that. In fact, I was there still when you summoned us all like so many underlings to attend to you. One minute I'm singing one of the old songs with my friends, the next we're all already outside without even knowing why, crossing the village with no cloaks to see what was so damned important that you had to use magic on all of us to accomplish it."

I felt my face flushing, and I was deeply embarrassed for what I had done. It had been excessive; I knew that now, but in the moment it had felt like an emergency. Plus, I was still so new to my powers.

But I said none of that. I wouldn't raise to his bait.

"So you and your brother have told me many times that I'm here as a witness and not a suspect," he said to Thorbjorn after giving up on waiting for me to respond.

"We have. And it's true," Thorbjorn said.

"And you told Roarr the same thing," he said to me. "And rumor has it you were at Loke's house, but you didn't summon him to pay court to you, so I guess he's not a suspect either."

"That's correct," I said.

"So tell me, do you have any suspects? Any at all?" He looked from me to Thorbjorn, then back again, raising an accusing eyebrow.

"Not yet," I said. "But the investigation is still in the early stages."

"I bet," he said. "Well, if it were me looking into things, I wouldn't be focusing on those like me that loved her beyond all reason. I would *never* hurt her."

"And you have an alibi," I said.

"Who do you think *would* hurt Nefja?" Thorbjorn asked.

"It's not that hard to figure out," Báfurr said, folding his arms over his chest like he was a professor waiting for us to work through some thorny problem on our own. But when neither of us spoke, he gave up with a dramatic roll of his eyes. "How many women have been chasing Roarr since Lisa died? Do you have any idea the number?"

"Not really," I said.

"All those women chasing him, for whatever reason," he couldn't resist adding. "But Nefja was far and away the most persistent." He sounded like he was proud of this fact. Like he admired her for it.

"You think someone thought she was going to succeed?" I asked.

"Everyone just saw the lengths Roarr would go to to get away from her."

"Not everyone was there last night," he said. "And she's been making her priorities clear for quite some time. It's not just her throwing herself at Roarr. It was her warning all the other women off. Maybe someone didn't like it. Maybe someone decided to get rid of her."

"Who?" I asked.

But Báfurr just shrugged. "All I'm saying is, there's a lot of women on a list of potential suspects you haven't even looked at, have you?"

"The number of women who could throw Nefja into that well is quite small," Thorbjorn said.

"Who said it was just one of them? Two women could do it. Or more. I would find it much more likely to be a woman than a man," he said, but then looked off with a bored air, thoroughly done with our conversation.

I tried to imagine the scene, two women sneaking up on Nefja and throwing her into the well before she knew what they were up to. It didn't seem likely at all.

On the other hand, he wasn't entirely wrong. In fact, I had a sinking feeling he was right about one thing. We weren't looking in the right direction at all.

CHAPTER SEVENTEEN

It was a relief to see the backs of Báfurr and his friends leaving my house. It was like an angry shadow was lifted from my home.

But it was still awkward as we all stood in my great room. All including Roarr, whom Thorbjorn and I really needed to have a discussion about, but not with him standing there.

"Coffee?" Kara offered, more to break the uneasy silence than because anyone looked like they needed more caffeine. But we all murmured a yes, and Nilda went with her into the kitchen.

"Ingrid," Roarr said.

I just barely avoided flinching. There was no way he knew what Thorbjorn and I were still stewing over, was there? "Yes?" I asked.

"I wanted to tell you that I saw Haraldr," he said. "You were still at Loke's house when I got back here."

"Right. Thanks," I said distractedly.

"Well," he said, all but squirming. "He wanted me to give you a message."

"Oh?"

"He said he will understand if you need to be late," Roarr said. "Late, but not absent."

"Am I supposed to be there now?" I asked.

"I don't *think* so," he said. "It was a little unclear. I rather hoped you'd just know what he meant."

"I've met him twice," I said with a sigh. "Wait, no. Three times. But still. I'm not familiar with his moods or basic personality or anything."

"You should see him as soon as you can," Thorbjorn said.

"But you and I need to..." But I broke off, leaving the end of that sentence unspoken.

Thorbjorn gave me the smallest of winks. "Roarr, why don't you go back to Haraldr and tell him you delivered his message. And Ingrid will be there for her lesson in... to be on the safe side, say within an hour."

"Sure," Roarr said, nodding. "Then come back here?"

"Well, if I'm going to be there, there'd be no reason for you to be here," I said.

"There must be some other task I can perform, then. I still want to help," he said.

"I know," I said. "Thorbjorn and I need to talk some things over before we decide what to do next. But once we know, we'll get in touch. If things are going to go the way they're looking to go, we're going to need a lot of help."

"Right," Roarr said. "I'll be at my house, so you'll know where to find me."

"Thanks," I said. Thorge got up from his chair to walk with Roarr to the front door, leaving me alone with Thorbjorn and a deeply sleeping Mjolner.

"You want to put him to work questioning his own girlfriends?" Thorbjorn asked, raising his eyebrows at me.

"First of all, he's been very clear none of them are his girlfriends. But aside from that, he doesn't have to know why anyone is on our list of suspects," I said.

"You don't think he'll figure it out?"

"Not if we only give him a few names. Maybe?" I sighed and rubbed tiredly at my face. "I don't want him to think this is just another backhanded way to make this all his fault. And seriously, you shouldn't call them his girlfriends. He never encouraged any of them."

"You're right," Thorbjorn said. "How do we draw up this list?"

"I know that one," I said, then waved for him to follow me back into the kitchen. Nilda and Kara were waiting for the coffee to brew, speaking with their heads close together. They both jumped when we walked in, and Kara flushed a pretty shade of pink.

"I have another job for you," I told them.

"They're going to know?" Thorbjorn asked.

"I rely on them implicitly," I said, and Kara flushed even darker at my compliment.

"They're going to know better than Roarr?" he pressed.

"Know what better than Roarr?" Nilda asked.

"We need a list of all the women who have been... expressing an interest in his company since Lisa died," I said. "Any amount of interest, large or small."

"Oh, we're totally the ones for that job," Kara said. "You think Roarr even notices who brings all the food to his house? He just scarfs it down and sets out the baskets for more."

"Oh, he's not that bad," Nilda said, giving her sister's arm a friendly punch. "But I agree, he couldn't tell you all the names. Not by a long shot. Especially if you're looking for the ones who are playing it a little more cool?"

"We need *all* the names," I said, and tried not to sound as exhausted as I felt. So many interviews, but they didn't have to start today.

The two of them immediately pulled a couple of chairs close together and started whispering names to each other, Nilda quickly filling a sheet of paper on both sides with name after name.

"Thorbjorn," Thorge said from the doorway, waving for his brother to join him in the hall. I watched the two whispering together, their faces grave. Thorge kept resting his hand on the hilt of his legionnaire's sword as he gestured with his other hand. My stomach was a hard knot long before Thorbjorn came back into the kitchen to tower over me.

"Ingrid, we have to go," he said. I had never seen him so serious. I swallowed hard.

"You said you'd be here until the end," I said. "Both of you."

"Something else has come up," he said. "It will require all five of us to deal with, and we must go at once."

"That sounds bad," I said.

"Nothing we haven't dealt with before," he assured me, but I could see the worry lines around his eyes again. "It does mean the passage to Runde will be sealed until we return."

"Okay," I said, not sure why he was telling me this, since I who was forbidden to take any way back to Runde, let alone the main one.

"You have your lesson with Haraldr, and then the three of you can start narrowing down that list of names," he told me. "I shouldn't think any of those interviews will be particularly dangerous, but listen to your gut. And if you need me, call."

"What happens if I call you?" I asked. "You can't be in two places at once."

"If you need me, call," he said, his hands gripping my shoulders almost painfully tightly.

"I will," I said. Then to my surprise, he planted a kiss on my forehead before joining his brother already waiting at my open front door.

And then he was gone.

Nilda and Kara were both watching me, their own task forgotten. I wondered how long they'd been watching and listening to us. But I couldn't focus on that. Instead, I slumped into a chair and stared at them helplessly.

"Tell me that doesn't mean he thinks he might die," I said. I tried for a joking tone, but my voice failed me.

"It looked pretty serious," Kara said. Her face was a neutral mask, which was an alarming change. Suddenly she had decided that I wasn't a person she could show emotions around? She, who had always been so open with everything?

It's not like it had even been a proper kiss.

Not like the one I hadn't quite shared with Andrew.

I groaned out loud and dropped my head down onto my folded arms on the table. My feelings about Thorbjorn were getting all mixed up with my feelings about Andrew, and somehow the only intelligible thought that made its way out of that morass was an angry blaming of the whole thing on Loke.

All he had done was see it first.

"Are you all right?" Nilda asked, gently touching her fingertips to my arm.

"Yeah," I said, sitting back in my chair and rubbing my face yet again. "I really need a nap. But I should probably get over to Haraldr's. Where did this whole day go?"

"We have a pretty good list," she told me, showing me the multiple sheets of paper. "It's expansive."

"We can start narrowing it down for you," Kara offered. "You can go see Haraldr, and will start talking to people for you."

"That would be so helpful," I said. "But be sure it doesn't seem like you're accusing anyone of anything."

"We were thinking we'd just ask people where they were last night," Nilda said, glancing over at her sister, who nodded her agreement. "Like a 'where were you when you heard the volva's call?' kind of thing. Maybe telling our version first."

"Catch people in groups," Kara added. "We thought that would be best, just for a first pass."

"Anyone who seems cagey or like there might be something going on there, we'll give their name to you to follow up," Nilda said.

"That sounds perfect," I said. "What would I do without you guys?"

Nilda smiled at me, but Kara's smile was just a shadow of its usual self, a mere tweak to that mask she was still wearing.

The two of them left to get changed before heading out to the mead halls at the dinner hour when they could find the most people together at once. I was left alone in my kitchen, looking at a full pot of coffee I was never going to drink.

My first thought was, how was I supposed to focus on runes with all this going on? It was such esoteric knowledge, far removed from what I needed to be doing now.

But maybe it would help, talking to Haraldr. Not about the case, but I was curious what he thought of my impressions of Loke's house.

Was it just the seeing Fe everywhere thing he had warned me about? Or was seeing it constantly inverted something else?

I washed up the plates and cups from the sandwich lunch, then dried and put everything away in the cupboards that still didn't really feel like mine. I was sure Nilda and Kara knew my kitchen better than I did at this point.

But finally I could delay it no longer. I got back into my coat and boots and headed out into the street to walk alone to Haraldr's house.

CHAPTER EIGHTEEN

WHEN I KNOCKED on the door, it was Haraldr himself who answered. He nodded at me, then wordlessly led me down the hall to the door to the library and then on to the still-cold fireplace. I settled onto my stool as he sat down on his.

Then we sat just looking at each other for an uncomfortable length of time. Was I supposed to speak first?

"I didn't make much progress," I admitted. I had only intended to break the silence, not lead with my failure, but there you go.

"It's only been a day," he said. "And it's the first rune you're attempting to bond with."

"It gets easier later on?" I asked.

He shrugged noncommittally.

"I haven't had a chance to do anything with it since I was interrupted last night," I said. "I was trying to draw the shape of the rune over and over, and it felt like I was getting close to something. I don't know, maybe I was almost about to have a breakthrough, and maybe I was almost about to realize I was kidding myself again. But I can't tell now. I was interrupted. I heard Nefja scream, and that's consumed me ever since."

"I can see that," he said. I gave him a puzzled look, and he nodded his head towards me. "You have dark circles under your eyes, and your hands have a slight tremor to them which I would chalk up to too much caffeine and too little sleep."

"That sounds about right," I said, looking down at my hands resting on my knees. They looked perfectly still to me, if a bit pale.

"But just because your conscious mind is focused on figuring out what happened to Nefja doesn't mean your subconscious mind isn't still ruminating on the meaning of the rune," he went on.

"That's true," I said. "Like you warned me, I keep seeing it."

"Everywhere?" he asked.

"Well, actually no," I admitted. "I saw it south of the village, when I was walking through the hills where the dairy cows graze."

"Ah," he said, nodding. "Well, you would see it there, wouldn't you?"

"I know," I said. "But I also saw it inverted."

"On the cows?" he asked with a frown.

"No, around Loke's house. And all over inside it," I said.

"Oh," he said. He was quiet for a moment, but in the end just nodded again. "Yes, that also makes a certain sense."

"How is that?" I asked. "Because they look down on their fortunes?"

"Not just that," he said. "You remember we spoke of hamingja before."

I nodded. "I guess their family has little of it."

"It has been dwindling in their line for generations," Haraldr said. "I had hoped that Loke's father would be the one to turn things around for them. For a while, when Loke was quite young, it looked like he would. But then there was the fire, and all that came after. Well, I'm not surprised you see inverted Fe all over their home. I fear they are coming to the end of their line."

"But surely there's something we can do to help?" I asked.

"Oh, no," Haraldr said, his tone shifting from bored academic to something more earnest. "If you think that you don't understand hamingja at all. Only Loke and his sister are left of their line. Any chance to change their hamingja is only on them. No one else can intervene."

"But that's so sad," I said.

"I know," he said, giving me a sorrowful half smile. "For centuries their line was one of the strongest in Villmark, rivaled only by your own and perhaps the ancestors of Valki's line. But everything that is created will eventually be destroyed."

"Oh," I said, sitting up straighter on my stool. It felt like an electric charge had just danced up my spine.

"Think of something else, did you?" he asked.

"It's just this thing with Nefja," I said. "I still don't know if she fell or was pushed or what. But the more I talk to people, the more I keep finding mismatched pairs."

"Pairs of what?" he asked.

"Of people," I said. "So many people in love with someone who is in love with someone else."

"A tale as old as time," he said with another sad smile.

"But it's still such a powerful thing," I said.

"I never said it wasn't," he said. "We've been talking about Fe as a rune of creation. In a very real sense, love is the thing that precedes creation."

"But it's also so destructive," I said.

"When it's inverted, yes," he said.

"Okay," I said. That made sense, maybe. But it didn't seem helpful. "If what we're saying is true, then why haven't I seen Fe reflected in any of the people I've been talking to? Isn't there a way to see who's love is going to turn to creation and whose to destruction?"

"My goodness, that would be a handy skill to have," Haraldr said. "But I can't imagine having such power."

"It doesn't sound impossible to me to learn to see like that," I said.

"Perhaps not, but for that I cannot be your teacher," he said. "My skills are not of that level."

"I understand," I said, but inside I was wondering if there was a way I could teach myself to do this thing. It would really simplify a lot of my investigations. Lisa had been killed out of twisted love ties as well. So had Gullveig.

"Fe is probably not the rune that will help you with this," he said, once again, as if reading my mind. "You've been seeing it with cows because its significance is more to do with wealth and prosperity than on human emotion."

"When do I learn the rest of the runes?" I asked. There had to be one that would help.

"One thing at a time," he said, laughing as he got up from the stool. At first I thought he was going to open the drawer that contained his rune bag, that we would go on to the second rune on the second day. But he walked further along the shelf, stopping at a cupboard door that he opened with a key.

"I have a gift for you," he said as he walked towards me with folds of suede cloth in his hands. "Not a gift from me, but something that was meant to pass down to you but fell into my possession for safe-keeping. This belonged to your ancestors, all the way back to Torfa herself, and before that time, who knows?"

He placed the suede on my knees and folded back the layers until I was looking down at an ornate necklace of amber beads shaped like teardrops. Each piece of amber was a slightly different shape and a slightly different color. I picked up the chain and let it dangle from my fingertips, then held it up to the light coming in from the south.

"It's gorgeous," I said. I wasn't lying, I really did find it incredibly beautiful. But it was a terrible sort of beauty. A woman wearing this was not a woman to be messed with. I could feel power radiating from it. Magical, but also something more. The power of matriarchs, maybe.

"It is yours," Haraldr said. "Do you understand the significance of it?"

"Freya," I said. "She had something like this in the myths, right?"

"When Freya was separated from her husband, she would weep. When she wept, those of her tears that fell to the earth became gold, but those that fell into the sea became amber."

"That's why they look like teardrops?" I asked.

"Perhaps," he said. "Amber floats, and it washed ashore where Torfa lived back in our ancestral lands. Perhaps that is the origin of the story. But whoever made this necklace likely chose the pieces of amber that looked most like teardrops to fit the story."

"So no one is thinking this is really Freya's necklace," I said.

"Brisingamen? Not hardly," he said.

"Was that also made of her tears?" I asked.

"That I don't know," he said, and look fell over his face, like he was remembering his own long-gone days of youth. "Would she wear a necklace of her own tears? Perhaps someday you can answer that question for me. But do you know why she cried?"

"Not really," I admitted.

"She missed her lover, Od," he said. "He was often away, and when he was away too long, she would walk the corners of the earth looking for him. And if she still couldn't find him, that was when she would weep."

"She treasured Brisingamen in a way that doesn't feel like it was a sad remembrance," I said. I could remember two different stories where it was stolen, and both times she had been angry in a way that only a goddess could get. But not bereft. "I can't imagine when I'd ever wear such a thing," I said regretfully as I laid it back down on the suede.

"You should wear it as often as you can at first, to establish a connection with it," he said. "You should especially wear it when you are meditating. The power of all of the volvas in your line is concentrated in that amber. That's power that you can learn to call on, should you ever need it."

I looked down on the amber beads resting on my lap and ran my fingers over their smooth surfaces. Had my grandmother worn this? Or her grandmother before her? Could I through these beads feel a connection to Torfa herself?

I closed my eyes and concentrated on the stones under my fingertips. I felt their age, I sensed the presence of their history, but I felt no connection.

My disappointment must have shown on my face because when I opened my eyes, Haraldr said, "just wear it and see what happens. You young people these days, so impatient. You realize the volvas with real power were all older than your grandmother is now? Such things can't be rushed."

"Of course not," I said. But I couldn't dismiss my impatience so easily. People needed me to have this power now. I was letting them down every day it took me to learn just another bit of knowledge. Such small bits, so many days.

Haraldr was watching me, and I knew he was waiting for me to put the necklace on, but instead I covered it back up in the folds of suede. Aside from having a power I couldn't access, I was sure that if I took it to an appraiser, I would find that it was worth more than my car, probably more than the house my mother and I had shared in St. Paul. It would feel really strange just wearing it around.

Not that I was likely to be mugged in Villmark or even in Runde. But still.

"I will wear it when I meditate," I promised him, and he sighed but nodded.

Then I went back outside, into a world that the mid afternoon sun had warmed to almost freezing, and trudged back to my house.

CHAPTER NINETEEN

MJOLNER WAS WAITING for me impatiently at the front door, and I immediately realized what I had forgotten to take care of when I had moved in.

There was no cat food here.

I went into the kitchen and found his dish in one of the cupboards, unpacked by either Nilda or Kara, I supposed. I filled the side for water and set it on the floor in the corner where he'd be out of the way. He didn't seem particularly thirsty, but took a few licking sips while I cut up some of the meat left over from the sandwiches to put in his bowl.

"Sorry," I said. "I'm not sure if you prefer this or kibble. I'll have to talk to Loke about bringing you something from Runde the next time I see him. Although, quite frankly, I'm sure Jessica would get the hint if you bugged her. She's pretty intuitive. In fact, she'd probably get you fish and chips if you played your cards right."

Mjolner gave me a meow, then started nibbling at the little pile of meat. He seemed satisfied, or at least willing to let it go for now.

I walked into my great room and looked at the sun setting over the southwestern hills. It really was an amazing view; I wasn't sure why my grandmother didn't like this place.

It still didn't feel like *my* home, but it was still new to me. I went up the stairs to my bedroom. I had now been wearing the same clothes for well past twenty-four hours, and a shower was very much in order.

It was wonderful to smell better, and clean hair is always a plus, but all that hot water made me sleepy. I went back into my bedroom and looked longingly at the bed. It was even angled to get none of the setting sun, perfect for late afternoon naps.

But it was past late afternoon now, and if I took a nap this late in the day, it would basically be bedtime for me and then I'd be up again at 4 a.m.

Plus, I was pretty sure I still had work to do. Maybe Nilda and Kara would want to talk over their progress. Or Roarr might come around looking to be assigned a task when he hadn't heard from me while waiting at home.

And there was always the possibility that Thorbjorn would come back from wherever he had gone.

No, I had to stay awake. But I didn't see that happening while I was alone in this big, empty house. So rather than pulling out something pajama-like, I dressed in clean going out clothes.

Before I pulled on my turtleneck, my eyes fell on the bundle of suede I had left on top of my dresser. I wasn't going to meditate now, that was another sure path to an early bedtime, and worse, one that happened on a rug somewhere. But it felt like it was time to start letting it rest against my skin. Under my turtleneck and heavy cardigan, no one would even know it was there.

There was no clasp, and it took a little work to get the ends tied together without getting my hair caught up in it. I imagined my ancestors would've left it on once they got it on.

But at last I managed to get it to hang evenly around my throat, the beads arranged around my neck like a radiating collar. It was imposing, but not remotely pretty. But then again, I had never been one to wear much in the way of jewelry.

I pulled my turtleneck on over it, then buttoned up my cable-knit cardigan. I could feel the beads pressed against my skin. Their initial coolness was slowly warming with the heat from my own flesh.

But I didn't feel any magical connection from it. It was just jewelry.

Maybe it would feel different when I actually *did* try meditating. But that sounded like a good thing to worry about in the morning.

I went downstairs and checked in on Mjolner, who was calmly washing himself after his meat feast. His water bowl was still full, and I could see in his green eyes that all he had planned for the evening was the nap I was forgoing.

I got into my coat and boots and headed out the door, towards Ullr's mead hall.

The last of the sun had just dipped under the crest of the hills when I reached the doors and let myself inside. Too early for most to be looking or dinner yet, although I half expected to find Roarr there.

He wasn't, but a mousy server emerged from the kitchen a shade too eagerly. Then her face fell when she saw it was me, or at least that I wasn't someone else.

I tried to remember her from the night I had been here eating with the others. I thought she might look familiar, but it was also possible I was just telling myself that. She was exactly the sort of person no one would really notice, not unless she had a big personality.

Her hair was some indeterminate shade between dark blonde and light brown, and her eyes were an unexceptional shade of blue, like the color had drained out of them.

But she was tiny, exceptionally so. And not just short but so thin I almost took her for a twelve-year-old girl. But I could tell she was older, perhaps my age or more. Her plain face had nothing left of the roundness of youth.

Still, I wondered how she managed to carry the heavy platters of meat I had seen moving around the room the other night, or to get her little hands around the handles of mugs full of ale. The other servers had come out of the kitchen with four or five mugs in each hand at a time.

Well, maybe that was why she worked the early shift. It required less lifting and carrying.

As I just stood there looking at her, her cheeks started to flush with embarrassment. She started to turn back to the kitchen, but I quickly said, "Bera, right?" She turned back to give me a wary look.

Then she remembered where she was and why and gestured to the room around us. "You can sit anywhere, I'll be right with you."

"Actually, I wanted to talk to you," I said. "That is, if you are Bera?"

"She's Bera," Ullr said as he came out of the kitchen with a bucketful of fresh charcoal for the grill in the center of the hall. "Bera, stay out here and talk with Ingrid Torfudottir. You have few enough duties yet, you can spare a moment for the volva."

"Uh, thanks," I said, still not comfortable with claiming that title. But correcting him with "volva-in-training" felt less than tactful.

Bera came back out of the kitchen with an almost sullen look on her face. Then she raised her hands to indicate the room around us. "Where?"

"This is fine," I said, heading to a spot on the far end of one of the long tables. Bera sat down next to me, but with plenty of space between us. Then she wiped her palms on the front of her apron and looked up at me.

"What can I help you with?" she asked.

"You were here last night, weren't you?" I asked. "When all the kerfuffle happened?"

"I don't remember a kerfuffle," she said evasively.

"Just a normal night working at the mead hall?" I asked and raised a single skeptical eyebrow at her.

"Well, maybe not normal," she allowed.

"You do know what happened after," I said.

"Yeah," she said. "But that was hours after. I don't see how it could be related at all."

"Why don't you just tell me everything you remember and leave how it's all related to me?" I said to her.

She nodded, then bit her lip as she collected her thoughts. "At first it was just Roarr here. He always comes early."

"You get on well with him?" I asked.

"He remembers my name. Most people don't," she said. "He looks me in the eye when he thanks me, and he's always polite even if he has to send something back."

"I worked in a diner for years," I said. "Those are all good qualities to have in a customer."

She looked up at me as if she thought I was teasing her, but after gazing into my eyes she gave a little nod. "It's hard work. A lot of nights, I don't even think it's worth it. But then there are the quiet evenings when Roarr comes, and I decide I can stick it out for a little bit longer."

"You have plans for pursuing other work?" I asked. I had no idea what the career possibilities in Villmark even were. Shopkeeper? Farmer's wife? There was so much I didn't know about this place, still.

"Something like that," she said noncommittally. "Anyway, last night wasn't quiet for long, because Sigvin brought her sister in. Usually they're fine, the two of them and Nilda and Kara. But Nefja was in a *mood*." She rolled her eyes.

"She was drinking," I said.

"No. Well, yes, she did drink when she was here, but she was in a mood before she even came in the door," Bera said. "Whatever set her off, I have no idea. She makes Roarr uncomfortable, you know."

"I do know," I agreed.

"Even on the best of nights, she bothers him in little ways. Last night, it was like she was deliberately trying to provoke him. I felt so bad for him. You know, after Loke came in and pulled Nefja away, I helped Roarr sneak out through the kitchen."

"I knew that was how he got away," I said, not mentioning that Sigvin had first taken credit for that escape. "But that wasn't all that happened. Báfurr and his friends came in here first."

Bera shrugged. "They aren't usually here, but they don't make trouble when they are. Not as friendly as Roarr, but they aren't rude either. Did someone tell you they made trouble last night? Because I don't think that's true at all. You might be listening to people who are telling lies."

"Nothing big like a fight," I admitted. "More like... bad feelings. Maybe you didn't notice."

She seemed to take offense at this, which I had meant just as an out for her. "I notice things," she said angrily. "I know that man Báfurr is smitten with Nefja. It's the only reason any of them come here. And she doesn't like him because she only has eyes for Roarr. And I'm not just talking about how she doesn't notice other men. I seriously don't think she has any kind of life outside of being obsessed with Roarr. I've noticed all those things."

"Okay," I said, holding up my hands, but she wasn't done yet.

"I know that Sigvin is drowning in quiet desperation, hoping that Loke will so much as look at her, but he never will. I know Kara is always watching the door in case Thorbjorn will show up. And he never does. But she is always watching all the same."

Then there was a gleam in her eye that I recognized at once. Loke got that gleam in his eye from time to time. It was the gleam of someone looking to start some trouble. "I even know who Thorbjorn is always looking for. Someone he's been looking for, for years and years. Oh, how he pines."

That gleam had tipped over into something like smug superiority. It turned her plain features into something more grim and even wicked. It wasn't pleasant.

I swallowed down the questions I wanted to ask and instead said, "you just told me he never comes in here."

"Practically never," she said with another dramatic roll of her eyes. "But I know what I know."

"Years and years, you say?" I said, my mouth suddenly dry. I almost raised my hand to get the attention of the server and ask for some water, but of course that server would've been her. I folded my hands together.

She was still gloating at me smugly, and I longed to summon the words to fight back.

But that wouldn't further my actual goals.

"How late were you here, last night?" I asked instead.

"The usual time," she said.

"And that is?" I pressed.

"Ten or so," she said with a shrug. "Then I walked home."

"And where's home?" I asked.

"South of the village," she said. Then that mischievous gleam was back in her eyes. "We're on the south side now, so you know as well as I that walk was through hills and trees, not up and down the streets here. And I was tucked away in my bed long before whatever happened to Nefja happened."

"And you know when that was, do you?" I asked.

"Everyone knows when that was. You called everyone out of bed," she said. "But I've heard the stories all day today, people complaining about the hour they were summoned out of bed. Luckily my parents and I live too far away to have been affected, or we'd be as sleep-deprived as you look."

The last shreds of my feelings of server solidarity flew away on the metaphorical wind. I really didn't like this woman.

"You live near Loke, then?" I said.

"Our house is near there, yes," she said. "But we own fields where we graze our dairy cows all around what's left of his estate."

"So when I walked to his house yesterday, those were your family's cows I was seeing?" I asked. Not adding, "the ones with the prosperity runes all over them?"

"Probably," she said.

"And your family is doing quite well?" I said.

"Oh, I see what you're saying," she said suspiciously.

"Really?" I said. I kept my tone neutral, but in fact I was surprised she knew when I didn't even know myself.

"You're saying that a rich young woman like me shouldn't be working in a place like this," she said.

"I assume you enjoy the work," I said. But then I remembered what she had been saying before. It had sounded like she didn't enjoy the work at all. She just enjoyed serving Roarr.

"I want a man who wants me for who I am, not what my family is worth," she said smugly.

I fought the urge to wish her good luck with that. Never in a million years would I point out to her that she was plain looking by any standards, Villmarker or modern. That might shrink the pool of

135

possibilities, but in my experience that was mainly getting rid of the shallow types.

No, what was going to stand in the way of her winning anyone's affections was her attitude. Her disdain for, apparently, all other women, and most of the men as well. Her smug superiority that didn't seem to have any base to rest on.

"There's been a debate whether Nefja fell or was pushed into the well," I said, watching her face carefully. But it betrayed nothing. She just waited for me to go on. "If she was pushed, it must've been by a man. Or by a group of women, maybe. But not a single woman. No woman could manage it on her own."

"Nefja was pretty drunk," Bera said. "But it would be tricky. They'd have to be strong, wouldn't they? Strong and tall. Taller than me. Or maybe they were just cunning."

"Cunning?" I repeated. "You think she was tricked into diving into that well?"

"I'm just saying, I work with cows. Cows are big. I know I'm just a tiny little thing, but even my dad who's big knows, if you're going to move a cow around, it's better to have their cooperation."

"Meaning?"

"It must've been someone she knew well. Someone she trusted."

I couldn't argue with that. It fit in too well with the shortness of the scream.

"Nilda and Kara are drawing up a list of suspects in Nefja's murder." I hit that word with a little extra emphasis to see how she would react, but she gave me nothing but a bored blink. "It's a list of women who were, as it were, courting Roarr."

Bera just shrugged as if such things didn't really interest her.

"Perhaps you know some names we can add," I went on. "You notice things, like you told me before. And you seem to have had a particular attention to Roarr. Maybe you've seen someone who was smitten with him that we might've missed."

"I doubt it. But, like I said, I'd look at her closest friends first. The people she trusted," she said. Then, although I had said nothing to dismiss her, she got to her feet.

"Well, give it some thought," I said. Then added on impulse, "It would be appreciated by Roarr, I'm sure. He's anxious to have this murder solved before suspicion falls on him. And he's told me before how very fond he is of you."

"He said that?" she asked, her brusque tone now an almost girlish whisper.

"Well, you always treat him so well when he comes in here," I said. "Why wouldn't he be fond of you?"

"Yes, I suppose," she said. Her cheeks were rosy, and there was a faraway look in her eyes. Like an innocent creature feeling the first, strongest pangs of love.

I almost laughed at the irony. If the Bera of five minutes ago could see herself now, what snarky comment would she use to cut herself down?

But it wasn't really funny, and I felt bad for implying that Roarr would ever return her interest. I wanted to undo that damage, but she was already gone, running back to the kitchen, and the front door was banging opening to let the first group of guests inside from the cold.

Which Bera was the true Bera, I wondered. The innocent girl or the bitter woman halfway down the path to spinsterhood?

And as she came out of the kitchen with several mugs full of ale in one of her tiny hands and a platter heaped with roasted meat balanced on the other, I wondered if such a slip of a thing could push anyone over the high walls of the well in the village commons.

She might have the will, but not the means. And I doubted very much with her attitude she had even a single friend who would help her do such a thing. Still, I wasn't ready to cross her name off the list just yet.

CHAPTER TWENTY

As I walked home I toyed with the idea of taking my sketchpad to the well and seeing what I could draw. But it was already dark, with clouds rolling in from the west, blotting out the dim stars above. Soon it would cover the moon, and there would be nothing but streetlight to draw by.

Maybe that would be enough. I would be looking in a magical way, not strictly a visual one.

But it was also getting colder by the minute. I didn't mind it so much so long as I was walking, my nose buried in the zipped-up collar of my parka, my mittened hands deep in my pockets.

But sitting still? And drawing? Which I couldn't exactly do in mittens. I could probably manage it in my thin driving gloves, but being thin those gloves didn't offer much in the way of warmth.

What if I sketched fast? Would that keep my hands warm enough? Would I get anything usable from the effort?

I didn't think I'd exactly reached a decision, but when I walked in my door I immediately took off my coat and boots, so maybe I had.

I still went to my drawing nook and looked at the charcoal drawings I had done the night before. I got tired just looking at them - they were a little hard to focus on - but it was still too early to sleep.

Meditation might be too soporific as well, but I had to try something. I built up a fire in the bedroom fireplace then once I had a couple of logs burning well enough not to need close tending, I sat down on the carpet in front of it. Eyes opened out of the darkness before me, in the shadows beside the light from the fire, and I jumped and almost shrieked, but of course it was Mjolner. He was in his upstairs cat bed, and gave me a little meow as if saying, "it's just me."

"You startled me," I said, and he meowed again then closed his eyes and went back to sleep.

I pulled off my turtleneck and sat in my camisole top, letting the light from the fire lick at the amber around my throat. I could see part of my reflection in the standing mirror near my dresser, and it was as if those beads were glowing.

Maybe this would work after all.

I closed my eyes and focused on my breathing.

I had never shifted into my magical perceptions so quickly. It almost snatched my breath away, but I just managed to keep it under my control. I could see living things like Mjolner glowing softly, the lights of those in the houses around me visible even through the walls between us. I could sense all of Villmark as well as an approaching snowstorm. Nothing major, but we'd probably have a few inches to shovel by sunrise.

I sensed all that, but I was getting nothing from the necklace itself. Slowly, I raised a hand and brushed my fingertips over the beads. I expected some answering sensation, but nothing came. It was completely inert to my attentions.

I focused my mind around a single thought: my desire to connect with my ancestors through this heirloom. Then I touched it again.

I still felt nothing from the necklace itself, but I barely noticed that because the sudden onset of sensations from all of Villmark around me barraged my magical senses.

So many people around me were seeking the same thing: a feeling of connection. With their families, with their friends, with unrequited crushes, some even with themselves. Not everything was to the same degree, but everyone had a little glow of dissatisfaction about how they were connecting with something.

Ironically, this amalgamation of feelings actually made me feel more connected to my fellow Villmarkers. They were not so tight knit as they appeared. Certainly not so closed off to outsiders as I had thought they were. They were slow to find me familiar, but I was still something new to them, and many of them had yet to even meet me.

But we were all a part of the same living network that thrived here, in a pocket between the present and the past. I might not yet feel connected to my ancestors, but I knew I had a present-day extended family all around me.

I was still basking in this glow of belonging when I felt something change, like we were all the surface of a pond in the warmth of summer and something, somewhere was causing ripples. I opened all my senses, but couldn't detect a source. Like the footsteps the night Nefja died, it seemed to come from everywhere, to be both very close and very far away at once.

But this disruption was moving through our collective selves through those gaps I had felt, the feelings of missed connections. Someone or something was using that, but for what?

I probed at the feeling of disruption and could tell little more about it, except that I felt an intelligence behind it. It was a someone, not a something, then.

And, as always, my mind went first to Halldis. Was she behind this?

I started to focus my attention downward, to the bedrock below the village and further down to the network of caves that lay beneath it. Except for the cavern that connected Runde to Villmark, the one that held our ancestral bonfire that had been burning since the first settlers came to these shores, I had never seen any of those caves. But I knew they were there, and that there were many of them, winding ever deeper into the earth.

Somewhere down there was Halldis, sealed in a cell both by a rock across the door and by my grandmother's protective wards. She couldn't get out physically, and she wasn't supposed to be able to influence anything outside her cell magically either.

But I had always had my doubts about that second part.

I couldn't tell if she was the source, but I turned my attention towards her. I let my consciousness sink into the ground beneath me. How far away were the caves? I sensed nothing around me but bedrock.

Then I sensed something around me. Or rather some things, separate minds that were swimming through the rock to reach me even though I was not a physical thing in that moment, just a consciousness.

There were five of them dancing all around me. I sensed them as dancing forms, something between a lizard or a salamander and a dragon. Two of them rushed up to either side of me and somehow started pulling me along, through the darkness of the bedrock to something that waited just before us.

Something like a bubble I could sense approaching, like my traveling consciousness had sonar and could trace out the shapes of things.

Not a bubble, a cell.

And within that cell, a being not like the creatures guiding me or the others still dancing around me. This was a human consciousness. It didn't know I was coming, but it would soon.

I wasn't a fool; I knew Halldis could sense me when I was in my magical meditative state. She had tried to reach out to me before. But I knew more now about my powers and how to protect myself. I was preparing for the moment when she would at last notice me.

Or I thought I was. But before I even got a chance to test myself, before my companions and I had even emerged from the bedrock into that cave, I was suddenly awake, eyes wide open, all too aware of being in my physical body. My currently very much in pain physical body.

I cursed as I scrambled back, thinking my thighs were on fire. Had the fire showered me in sparks? It didn't seem likely, and even if it had, the pain I was feeling was more than a few airborne embers finding their way to me and burning through my leggings. Still I beat at my own legs to put out any flames.

Then there was a yowl and I realized what I was slapping at wasn't fire. It was Mjolner. Not only was he on my lap, he had sunk his claws deep into my thighs. My pants were completely ruined, and blood was oozing from long scratches that were already turning flame red.

"Mjolner!" I gasped.

He meowed at me as if annoyed and then flounced out of the room with his tail up at its most bristly and angry.

Why had he done that?

I went upstairs and into the bathroom and searched through the cabinets until I found cotton balls and rubbing alcohol. I regretted not finding a bullet to bite down on first as I swabbed at my wounds. The pain was sudden and exquisite. But cat scratches are nothing to mess around with.

I didn't know half the places Mjolner went. I had no clue what could be on his paws. He might have just exposed me to some magical toxins. But the ordinary kind were problematic enough.

I took a deep breath and washed each of the scratches again, then went back into my bedroom to change into my pajamas.

The throbbing in my thighs started to abate, and the heat of the skin was settling down, and by the time I climbed into that overly large bed I realized my anger had faded as well.

The only reason Mjolner would have done something like that was to save me. I knew that from past experience. And as much as I suspected that he could talk if he chose to, he had never yet chosen to. So he couldn't exactly tell me what he thought he had just saved me from.

Halldis, again? That seemed likely.

Only, she hadn't done anything. I had specifically gone looking for her, but I had no sense that she had even been aware of me, let alone waiting for me to fall into some magical trap.

Of course if I had been about to fall into a trap, I wouldn't have known it. Or else it wouldn't have been a very good trap. I wouldn't have needed Mjolner's help to evade it.

The companions who had surrounded me had seemed helpful. But what if they had been guiding me towards bigger trouble?

My last thought before sleep finally claimed me: there might be more than one danger lurking in Villmark.

CHAPTER TWENTY-ONE

I woke the next morning to a pounding at my front door, and the vague feeling that this pounding had been going on for some time. The sky to the east was lightening, but it was still long before sunrise.

There was an irritated meow from behind my head. Mjolner, who had two beds of his own now, was in his customary spot: the very middle of my pillow, curled up against the back of my neck. He meowed again, as much as demanding that I go get the door and let him finish sleeping in peace.

For my part, I felt fully rested. My brain was sharper than it had been in days, and the aches and pains I hadn't even been aware of before were suddenly gone.

I reached for my robe and slipped my feet into my fur-lined slippers before heading downstairs. The house was colder than my grandmother kept her cottage, and I was grateful for the thick shawl collar of my robe as I snugged it tighter around me before pulling open my front door.

I couldn't see his features, but there was only one person who would knock on my door at that hour and who stood so tall and so broad.

"Thorbjorn," I said. "I thought for sure it would be days before I saw you again. Come in."

He came inside without a word, and I shut the door behind him then reached for the lightswitch.

He was covered in snow. It rested in little drifts on his shoulders and was frozen to his eyebrows and beard.

But something else was matted in his hair.

"Is that blood?" I asked, rising up on tiptoe to try to get a better look.

"It doesn't matter," he said. He sounded beyond exhausted, and he was moving so slowly and so stiffly I had to help him get out of the layers of the cloak he wore over his wool coat.

"Are you hurt?" I asked.

"Just tired," he said. "And hungry. Do you have anything to eat?"

"Come into the kitchen and I'll make you some steak and eggs," I said.

"Perfection," he said, although he didn't sound as enthused as the word warranted. And when he bent to take off his boots he suddenly stumbled back against the wall, clutching at his forehead.

"You *are* hurt," I said. "Sit down on that bench before you fall down."

"Ingrid-" he started to say, waving me away, but I was firm.

"If you fall down on me you're going to crush me, and then where will we be? Sit down."

He gave in with a nod, a motion that seemed to make him queasy as his cold-reddened face shifted to a shade of green. I pulled off his boots one at a time then held out a hand to help him back to his feet.

"Were you and your brothers fighting trolls again?" I asked as I pushed him down the hall, into the kitchen, and then into one of my kitchen chairs.

"Trolls are fun," he said. "This was giants."

"Giants are more aggressive?" I asked as I got coffee going before taking down one of my cast iron frying pans.

"Very," he said, delicately probing at his hairline and wincing slightly.

"If you have a head injury, I should call someone," I said.

"It's been seen to," he said.

"By whom? One of your brothers?" I asked.

"I'm okay. Or I will be. I've had worse," he ended lamely.

"If you got back here so fast, does that mean the giants were close?" I asked.

"Yes. Hence the emergency," he said. "But it's been dealt with. I am once more at your disposal."

"I'm thinking I should dispose you back at your house so you can get some sleep and heal up," I said.

"Eggs first, please," he said.

"Coming up," I said. "You came straight here, didn't you? You were covered in snow like you walked all night through the storm."

"It wasn't much of a storm, really," he said. "And I actually went home first to drop off my weapons."

"But you didn't really stop there," I said.

"I spoke to my father," he said. "He told me what Brigida learned from Nefja's body."

That got my attention. I turned my back on the stove to look at him. "Wait, she can do forensics?"

"Nothing like that," he said. "But she did say there was no sign of a fight. Nefja struck the very top of her skull on the ice, but that could have come from a fall."

"So what she was really saying was that she thought this was an accident," I said.

"She said she thought that was the most likely interpretation of the evidence," Thorbjorn said. "Have you learned anything more? Anything that proves it was murder?"

"Not really," I said, turning back to put a steak on the now piping hot pan. It hissed and sizzled the moment it touched that iron. "Nilda and Kara were going to do some preliminary investigations of all of the women who were expressing an interest in Roarr since Lisa died. They were going to report back to me."

"But they didn't?"

"Well, I fell asleep early, and slept quite hard," I said. "It's possible they stopped by and I just never heard them."

He snorted but said nothing. He had probably been knocking for a lot longer than I thought he had.

"We should talk to them before we make any decisions," he said after a moment. "But if we've really run out of leads, and with nothing more to work from, maybe it's time to call this an accident and let everyone move on. The idea that it was a coalition of jilted women just isn't feeling true to me."

"So the person running away we'll just chalk up to coincidence?" I asked as I scrambled some eggs and poured them into the other side of the pan.

"You heard a person running," he reminded me. "You said you couldn't tell the direction. So how do you know it was away from the scene of the crime?"

"A feeling," I said.

"All else being equal, I'm inclined to trust your feelings," he said, but I could tell he was being carefully diplomatic.

"But?" I prompted as I poured out two mugs of coffee.

"Well, it's not much to go on. What more can we do?"

"I was going to go back to the well today and try sketching there," I said.

"You haven't done that yet?" he asked.

"No," I said, rather defensively. "Look, I've been doing magic every day since I got here. Haraldr wanted me to bond with a rune and then bond with a necklace, and neither of those things really worked out. And then I *did* feel connected to everyone in the village, which was actually kind of nice, only there was this other thing that was disrupting all those connections, and..."

I had been talking way too fast, my words tumbling over each other as I plated up the steak and half of the eggs. But it was still startling to see Thorbjorn gaping at me when I turned to hand that plate to him.

"What?"

"What are you talking about?" he asked. "Something was disrupting something, what does that even mean?"

"I was meditating last night," I said, turning back to plate up my own eggs. "A Haraldr assignment. Only I didn't feel what I was supposed to."

"I'm not sure there is a supposed to with these things," he said around a mouthful of food.

"I know," I said. "I just wish things were clearer sometimes, you know? It's like I'm trying to see the outlines of a watercolor sketch after someone left it out in the rain. How do I know what was originally there and what I'm just making up in my own artistic mind?"

"You think you were making things up?" he asked.

"I would if not for Mjolner," I said.

"Back up. Explain."

"Well, I felt this disrupting influence, like something malignant was hiding here among us, moving through us using the feelings of people about each other, the negative feelings. Like isolation and loneliness. But it was all so vague that, again, I would think I was imagining it, only I was pulled out of that trance quite suddenly by Mjolner digging every one of his claws into my thighs and tearing great gashes in my skin. And then just walking away like I was the one who had done something wrong."

"Where is he now?" Thorbjorn asked.

"Upstairs, sleeping," I said, then took a bite of my eggs.

"I agree if he reacted that way, you were likely in more danger than you knew," he said.

"I thought maybe it was Halldis," I said. He raised a skeptical eyebrow at me. "I know, I know. I'm the girl who cried Halldis. Only I really don't think I'll ever feel safe until I can see for myself that she is bound."

"I could take you down there, if you like," he said.

"That doesn't break the rules?" I asked.

He just shrugged.

"I don't think I should," I said with a sigh. "Because that thing about knowing she is bound before I feel safe? I don't know how to even tell such a thing yet. I still have so much to learn."

"I can see why that might make you feel unsafe," he said. "If it helps, I can already see how much you've changed since you came back to us just a few months ago. Your power has grown immeasurably in what is really a very short period of time. It's like you glow."

"Well, thanks," I said. I felt my face flushing and concentrated on my eggs.

"That's helped," Thorbjorn said as he pushed back his spotlessly empty plate. "Thank you. I am prepared for the next task."

"A long nap and then more food?" I suggested.

"Later," he said with a wave of his hand.

"What about that gash on your forehead?" I asked.

He pulled back his hair to show me a row of immaculate stitches, perfectly even.

"Did you put some antibiotic on that?" I asked.

He laughed. "You nag like your grandmother when you choose to, you know that?"

"That's not an answer," I said. "I have supplies in my bathroom upstairs. Get some antibiotic cream on there and then put a bandage over it. The last thing that wound needs is your hair getting into it before it's closed up."

"Understood," he said. "What are you going to be doing?"

"First, getting dressed," I said, and drank down the last of my coffee.

"And then?"

"Then I'm getting my sketchbook out and heading to the well. Which I really should've done yesterday, but I was just so sure this hadn't been an accident," I said.

"You think now that it was?" he asked.

"I think now that I should've at least checked," I said. "Hopefully whatever I draw, when I look at it I'll be able to tell if it was an accident or murder. And if it *was* a murder, where I should be looking next."

"I think you won't need me for any of that," he said. "When I've bandaged my head I'm going to find Nilda and Kara and find out what they've learned."

"Good plan," I said. "We'll meet back here afterwards."

He nodded and then followed me up the stairs. I pointed out the bathroom to him then went into my bedroom, but turned back before closing the door.

"Thorbjorn?" I called.

He poked his head back out into the hall.

"I'm glad you're all right," I said. "But I'm getting the full story later, right? The story about what happened with the giants?"

"You'll be getting that tale in five part harmony before this night is out, that I can promise you," he said. Then he disappeared into the bathroom again and I went to put on my warmest clothes.

CHAPTER TWENTY-TWO

THERE WERE benches arranged around the perimeter of the village commons, all facing the well in the center, but as I was packing up my art supplies I decided they were too far away for what I wanted to do. I looked around the great room and saw a three-legged stool sitting near the fireplace, opposite Mjolner's cat bed. It would be easy enough to carry down the street. I slung my bag over my shoulder and hoisted up the stool then headed back outside.

The sky was cloudy and the newly fallen snow in my front garden was nearly taller than my boots. I would have to figure out where I had a shovel at some point. In the meantime, I muscled my front gate open despite the barricade of snow and stumbled out into the street.

The snow was gone on my end of the street, but when I looked down the road to the south I could see a handful of people still working their way along, shoveling snow onto the backs of sledges to be hauled out of the village. I supposed if the village were any bigger, someone would've figured out a way to get a plow truck up from Runde.

The old-fashioned method looked tedious, but the people doing it didn't seem to mind. They were singing a song that sounded familiar, probably one of the ones I had heard when we had been out on the

Viking ship in the fall. The rhythms that had then kept everyone rowing together were now coordinating the shoveling. It looked like something out of a musical, all the snow arcing through the sky in time.

They must have started at the center of town, because the way I needed to walk was entirely clear. I walked up to the well and set my stool on the ground but didn't sit down right away. Instead I walked around the well, running my gloved hand over its stone walls. Nothing was sparking any magical impressions, but the artist in me picked an angle to start drawing from pretty quickly.

I moved my stool to where I wanted it and set my bag on the ground beside it. Then I sat down, took out my sketchbook and pencil, and got to work.

It was awkward as anything, drawing with gloves on, but the air was so cold I kept my chin tucked low so I could breathe inside the collar of my parka where the chill in the air wasn't quite so painful. My hands were already feeling the numbing effects even with the gloves on.

I was going to have to work quickly.

I put my pencil to paper and started sketching, quickly filling the page then turning to a fresh one to start again. I kept drawing, page after page, but between the sense of hurry and the frostbite nipping at my hands, I just couldn't get into the process deeply enough to get into the flow.

I put down the book and my pencil and blew on my gloved hands and rubbed them together. I needed to try something else.

Then I remembered my grandmother's light spell. I always used it to make light when I needed it, but it was really a fireball. It would give off heat too, wouldn't it? If I held on to it rather than casting it up into the sky, could it keep my hands warm?

I tried it, creating the little ball then holding it on my palms. It glowed brightly, and I could feel the warmth of it through my gloves.

But I couldn't exactly draw while holding on to fire.

Or could I? It was magic fire. Maybe it wouldn't burn paper. It certainly wasn't burning my hands.

But it did take up space. I suppose I could keep switching hands...

Only that would mean I would be drawing with no hands on the sketchbook. It would have to just rest on my knees. Not ideal.

I looked down at the ball of light, and without even questioning what I was doing I dug my thumbs into it, like I was pulling the sections of an orange apart.

It split in two, but before I could even wonder what I could try next, those two halves just melted into my palms. I gave a little cry of disappointment, but I hadn't broken it at all. It was there still, it was just out of sight. I could feel its warmth inside my gloves now. I held my hands up closer to my eyes and could just see a little glow coming out of the cuffs of my gloves.

It had known what I wanted.

This time when I started sketching, it only took a few minutes for the work of making lines became the flow of creating art. I don't know how long I kept it up, filling even more pages until I reached the end of my sketchbook and had to stop.

I blinked and looked around. It was hard to tell how much time had passed with the sun lost behind clouds, but I had filled half a sketchbook with images, so it must have been hours.

I put the book and pencil away in my bag then picked up my stool to carry it back home. I was suddenly very hungry.

When I got home, there was no sign of Thorbjorn or Mjolner. I made myself a cheese sandwich then sat down at the kitchen table to turn through the pages of my sketchbook while I ate.

I started at my first attempts, before I had cast the heat spell. They were perfectly nice drawings of a well, but no more than that.

Then I got to the latter set of drawings, and they too were all just the well, no hidden clues or images like the boats I had drawn where Gullveig had died.

What there was, however, was the Fe rune absolutely everywhere. It was worked into the pattern of the stone, it filled the cloudy sky beyond. In the pictures where I had put in the buildings that bordered the square, it was repeated all through their architecture as well. Some were faint but most were darkly defined, not subtle at all.

I shut the book with a sigh. Haraldr had warned me, but I don't think either of us had appreciated just how suggestible my mind was. Not only was I seeing Fe everywhere, I wasn't seeing anything else.

Fe couldn't tell me if this was an accident or a murder. It couldn't tell me if anyone was responsible, or if there had been a witness to the actual event.

It couldn't tell me anything. But it wouldn't stop trying to talk to me.

A sudden weariness settled on me. I wasn't physically tired, not after my epic night of sleep, but I was mentally exhausted. I was tired of trying to do things I didn't seem to be capable of grasping even the basics of.

And I really, really missed my friends down in Runde. It had only been a few days without them. How was I going to make it for however long I was expected to?

A little voice at the back of my head wanted to remind me that I could quit anytime I wanted to, but I squelched it hard before it could even form the words.

Quitting wasn't an option. My grandmother needed me. The people of Villmark were going to need me someday soon.

And Nefja's family needed me now. They needed to know what really happened to her, and no one else was going to be able to find out for them.

I would just have to keep trying.

But just bullheadedly doing the same thing over and over wasn't going to help anything. I needed to take a different tack. But I had no idea what to try. I needed an outside-the-box idea, but I wasn't particularly good at those. Not when it came to magic.

But I knew someone who was.

The minute I thought his name, I got up from the table and stuffed my sketchbook back into my bag. I scrawled a quick note for Thorbjorn or Nilda and Kara or whoever else might come by looking for me.

Then I got back into my winter things to head down the hill to Loke's house.

CHAPTER TWENTY-THREE

THERE MUST BE some sort of etiquette rule regarding how many times you can knock on someone's door before just accepting that they are either not home or have no intention of answering. I don't know what that number is myself, but I'm pretty sure I exceeded it.

There's probably also an etiquette rule regarding the volume of those knocks. If so, I broke that as well.

But I didn't want to just turn around and walk back home. The answers to my questions weren't going to be found there. I put my hand on the doorknob and gave it a testing turn.

My heart was in my throat as I did this. What was I going to do if I found that it wasn't locked? Was I really going to emulate my grandmother and just let myself in to someone else's house? My skin crawled at the mere thought.

So it was kind of a relief when the knob refused to turn. Like Loke being the complete opposite of everyone else in Villmark was saving me from myself.

But that still left me with my original quandary. Should I wait on the porch for him to come home, or give up and walk back to town?

I turned towards the road and looked around. I didn't want to admit to myself I was hoping my cat would appear to lead me to where I needed to be, but I knew that was what I was doing.

But he wasn't there. The only living things I could see were the cows that stared unblinkingly at me from the other side of the fences that flanked the house. Bera's family's cows. At least this time the Fe rune wasn't jumping out at me everywhere I looked.

Maybe my sketching had gotten it all out of my system. In which case, it hadn't been a *complete* waste of time.

I stepped down off the porch, but rather than head back to the road I walked along the outside of the house, peeking into the windows as I passed them. Most of them showed me nothing but folds of heavy drapery faded from years of sunlight and fuzzy with dust.

Then I reached another door. Had there been a back door out of the kitchen? I searched my memory, but as dimly lit as the interior of the house had been, I couldn't be sure if I had missed seeing one. But this door seemed to line up with my sense of the geography of the house and where the kitchen was.

My hand closed around the doorknob of its own accord, but the minute I realized what it was about to do I stumbled back, slipping on the snow, clutching my hand to my stomach like I was trying to control a thing suddenly possessed.

My grandmother was a really bad influence.

When I had myself under control I stepped back up to the door and knocked on it gently. Surely no one would answer. No one had answered the front door. But just as I started to move on to the next window, I saw the doorknob turn.

The door opened only the narrowest of cracks, enough for me to see one blue eye peering out at me. "Ingrid?" Esja said.

"Sorry, did I wake you?" I asked.

"No, I was just lying down," she said. The eye looking out at me was blinking and watering, and I realized that even this overcast day was likely too bright for her.

"I'm sorry. I didn't mean to disturb you," I said.

"Don't be silly. Come in," she said, stepping back into the shadows but leaving the door standing open.

I doubted the chill would do her any good, so I rushed inside and shut the door behind me. Then I stood blinking, waiting for my eyes to adjust. "I needed to talk to Loke about something," I said, directing my words to the general direction I thought Esja might be in.

"He's not home at the moment," Esja said. "Would you like some tea? You look so cold. Your cheeks are the most alarming shade of red."

"I don't want to be any trouble," I said. "Do you know when he'll be back?"

"I so rarely do," she said. "I was just about to have a little tea myself, so it's absolutely not any trouble. You can hang your coat on that hook behind you then come over by the stove where it's warmer."

"All right," I said. She had an awfully practiced tone to her bossiness for someone who only ever talked to her older brother. I hung up my coat and stepped out of my snow-laden boots then joined her at the kitchen table.

"Shortbread?" she offered. "It's my favorite, but it has caraway seeds in it. Some people find that off-putting."

"Some people being Loke, I'm guessing?" I asked as I helped myself to one of the squares. It had been baked in a mold and had a pattern pressed into it like a sheaf of grain. I could see the seeds inside it, little dark flecks in the otherwise rich, buttery cookie. I took a bite. "That's actually quite good."

"Truly?" Esja asked, giving me a nervous smile.

"I never lie about liking food," I told her. "I can't stand eating things I don't like just to be polite."

"Does that happen?" she asked, resting her chin on her hands. "Is that something friends do, or family?"

I supposed that she had neither, aside from Loke, but it still struck me as a deeply sad question. "Both," I told her. "My mother used to make this casserole that was supposed to be like ratatouille only it was so, so watery. Maybe she was making it wrong. But she was so anxious to know what I thought the first time she tried out the recipe that I told her it was good. Somehow that morphed into this casserole being my favorite thing, at least in her head. She made it every year on my birthday!" I laughed and shook my head at the memory.

Esja smiled then got up to take the whistling kettle off the stove. "What happened when you told her the truth?" she asked.

"I confess, I never did," I said. "I had it for my birthday last year, in fact." A sudden horrible thought struck me. "What if I start craving it? Like my birthday isn't really my birthday without it? What if I feel compelled to try to recreate it?"

"Well, you can always tinker with the recipe until it tastes right to you," Esja said diplomatically as she poured water into two mugs with teabags already in them.

"I suppose," I said.

"So," Esja said as she came back to the table with the tea. "What did you need to talk to Loke about? It seemed important, and you never know. Maybe I can help." She looked at me expectantly as she bit into a square of shortbread.

"I'm not sure you can," I said.

"Is it about Nefja?" she asked.

"He's told you about that?" I asked. She just shrugged. "Well, it's related to that, but not entirely."

"You like being mysterious," she said with a teasing glint to her eye.

"I'm supposed to be learning magic. So I can maybe someday be the next volva. Only I'm not making much progress," I said.

"That's not what I've heard," she said.

"Loke is being kind," I said.

"Who said I heard that from Loke?" she said and took a sip of tea.

"Who's being mysterious now?" I asked, and she laughed.

"I'm afraid I don't know anything about magic," she said. "But I'm not sure how Loke could help you either. Not with volva magic."

"I actually needed a different perspective on the problem, and he's very good for those," I said.

"He is at that," she said with a fond smile. "I really wish I could help you, but I honestly have no idea where he is or when he'll be back. He just comes and goes. Especially on days like today where I feel stronger, he's here less."

"That must be terribly lonely for you," I said.

"Well, you're here now," she said. "But mostly I don't really mind. People can be very exhausting. And before you start apologizing again, I don't mean you. You're perfectly lovely."

"Drinking your tea and eating your cookies," I said sarcastically.

"Yes, and telling me about your work," she said as if I had been speaking seriously. "I like talking about things that aren't me and how I'm feeling, you know?"

I knew exactly what she meant. My mother had been the same way. She had been sick for as long as I could remember. For most of my life, she had known that she was going to die young. But she hadn't wanted to dwell on it. She had wanted to laugh over movies together or pore over my artwork with careful attention.

"Maybe you *can* help me, actually," I said and went back to where I had left my bag by the door. "I've been drawing, that's how I can best interact with my magic. Usually it gives me clues, although they aren't always easy to find. But today I didn't seem to get anything at all. And yet when I was drawing, I felt in touch with that magic. So not seeing anything now is pretty odd."

"I'd love to look at your art," she said eagerly.

"Well, this isn't so much art in its finished form as me sketching the same well over and over again," I said.

"I'd still like to see it."

I brought the sketchbook over to her and opened it to the first page from that morning.

"You sit there and drink your tea while I look," she commanded me without looking up from the page.

She was very good at that bossy thing. But I did as I was told. I sipped the rest of my tea and ate another piece of shortbread as she turned the pages one after another. She lingered on some sketches longer than others, but I couldn't tell why. Her face was always so carefully neutral.

"You were trying to find out what happened to Nefja?" she guessed when she had at last reached the last page and had closed the book.

"Yes, but as you can see all I'm getting is the Fe rune over and over again," I said. "That's from a lesson I've been doing with Haraldr. He's teaching me rune magic one rune at a time, and that's literally the only rune we've done."

"Oh," Esja said and opened the book again to look at the sketches. "Oh yes. I see what you mean."

"You didn't notice it the first time?" I asked, incredulous.

She looked up at me. "Are you kidding? I was supposed to notice something as subtle as a three-stroke rune when these pages are covered in cows?"

I gaped at her. Was she crazy? Was she having a joke at my expense?

But she was completely serious. She frowned at my expression then turned the book around and pushed it across the table towards me. "Look," she said.

I looked.

She was right. There were cows everywhere. Sometimes a full body cow, sometimes just the head of a cow. They weren't drawn in definite lines, they were more something that emerged from the patterns in the shading. But as I turned the pages I saw they really were absolutely everywhere, even on the first drawings.

"How did I miss this?" I asked myself.

But it was Esja that answered, "because you saw the Fe everywhere and stopped looking?"

"I think you're right," I said. "But what could cows mean besides just another way of indicating the rune Fe?"

"To paraphrase something I've read, sometimes a cow is just a cow," she said. She picked up her mug but found it empty and set it back down with a little pout of disappointment.

"Do you know Bera?" I asked suddenly. "I don't know her family name, but I think she lives near here?"

"I've seen her on occasion," Esja said. "She lives with her parents and her brother just a little further to the south. If you go back out to the road, it's around the next hill."

"Thanks," I said and got up from my chair.

"You think cows means Bera?" she asked, turning in her chair to watch me as I pulled my boots back on.

"I think maybe it means she was there," I said.

"You think she pushed Nefja into the well?" she asked. "She's so little. It would be like... well, me pushing someone into a well. Aren't the walls awfully high?"

"She's stronger than she looks," I said. "But if she didn't do it, she was there. She saw something. And if she did, she never told me about it. So who is she covering up for?"

"That's a horrid thought," Esja said.

"Tell me about it," I said. "I hate where my mind goes. I didn't use to think this way."

"Not before you started solving murders," she guessed.

"I think you're right about that," I said.

"If you're going to confront her, you should bring someone with you," she said. "Not me, of course, but someone. How I *do* wish my brother were here."

"I'm not going to confront her," I said.

"Then what?"

"I'd like to talk to her parents about her. I want a better grasp of things before I try talking to her again. She's... difficult."

"Well, good luck," Esja said.

"Thanks," I said. "And I swear, as soon as I get the chance, I'm going to bring you some of my actual art."

"I look forward to it," she said with a smile.

Then I was gone, trudging back up the path as fast as the heavy snow would let me.

CHAPTER TWENTY-FOUR

I TRUDGED BACK out to the main road, then followed Esja's directions, turning south and continuing on around the next hill. That hill was a low but wide mound, and the road swerved far to the east to get around it.

It wasn't a short walk. I had a lot of time to think, but my thoughts just ran in circles. Báfurr loved Nefja. Nefja loved Roarr. But Roarr loved only Lisa.

Was Bera just fond of Roarr, or was she in love as well? Did she do more than watch everything that happened in the mead hall and carry her little grudges? She had seemed so quiet, but once I had gotten her talking, the words had just gushed out of her, and a lot of them had been heated.

Was her near invisibility hiding something besides shyness as well?

At last I came around the hill, and the farmhouse came into view. It was neither modernist like the houses in town nor Gothic like Loke's family's home. It was more like a typical Minnesotan farmhouse from the early 1900s. Very square, very modest, and currently buried under a heavy layer of snow. The walls were horizontal planks of gray wood, the windows tiny and irregularly spaced. It was built in an L-shape, and I suspected an addition had been built onto a more rectangular original structure.

Like with Loke's house, the fenced-in cow pastures were close on either side of me as I approached the house. But the space between was wider here, containing not just the house but a complex of buildings arranged in a semicircle.

To the left of the open yard that was the heart of the semicircle and set just a bit further back than the house was a separate garage. But this wasn't scaled for cars but for farming equipment. I could see the tracks left by massive truck tires in front of the now-closed doors.

At the back of that circular yard and extending beyond both of the front two buildings was a long, low-roofed structure I guessed was for housing the cows at night and milking them in the morning. But those cows must go in and out through the back, as there were no signs of them from where I was standing.

The yard was trampled with crisscrossing footprints, humans of varying sizes, but the walk up from the road was marred only by the same small tracks going back and forth.

So Bera went into town, but the rest of the family stayed on the farm? Or else they all had tiny feet like Bera. But I examined them as I walked beside them, and I was pretty sure all the tracks were from the same boots.

I stepped up onto the covered porch that filled in the missing corner of the L to so that the whole house formed a square. A pair of chairs were arranged around a little table, and there was a swing on the very far end of that porch, but everything was covered with several inches of undisturbed snow. But the side of the porch closest to the front door was swept clean to the floorboards, and I stomped the snow off my boots at the top of the stairs before walking up to the front door to knock.

A woman opened that door, and at the same instant a man emerged from the barn to cross the yard. The woman was as short as Bera, but much rounder. Her dark gray hair was pulled back from her face into a bun at the nape, but a single curly lock had escaped to hang over her forehead.

I couldn't tell much about the man, who had a wool hat with long earflaps pulled down low over his eyes and the collar of his modern-looking winter coat zipped up to his nose, save that he was tall if not so broad in the chest as most Villmarker men were.

"Hello," I said, glancing from the woman to the approaching man and back again. "You're Bera's parents?"

"That's right," the woman said. She put out her hand for me to shake. "I'm Lifa. That there is my husband Falr. What can we do for you, Ingrid Torfudottir?"

"I wanted to talk to you about Bera, if that's all right," I said.

"She's not home at the moment," Lifa said. "She's already gone up to the village."

"She works this early in the day?" I asked.

"No, not usually," Lifa said. "I think she had something else to do. I didn't ask. Would you like to come in?"

"Yes, thanks," I said, coming into the house. There was no separate mud room, but there was an area by the door with hooks for coats and a mat for boots. I took off my coat and hung it up, then pulled off my boots as Falr beside me did the same.

I saw now that he had a thick head of hair that stood straight up after he took his hat off. The dark gray color was a match for his wife's. He wore overalls of a thick, warm-looking black cloth over a hand-knit sweater, and I doubted he had felt a bit of the cold anywhere except for the tip of his very red nose.

"Coffee?" Lifa called from the kitchen, which was separated from the main room by a long waist-high countertop.

"Yes, please," Falr and I said together, and he laughed. We crossed the tidy living room to gather in the kitchen.

"So, you know who I am," I said as I took the warm mug Lifa brought to me. "Do you know why I'm here?"

"No," Lifa said. "Except you said you wanted to talk about Bera."

"Hardly surprising," Falr said, then took a long swallow of his own coffee. I didn't know what to make of his words. His tone was far too mild-mannered for him to suspect I was there because of a murder.

"You've been expecting me, then?" I asked. Lifa made a gesture, and we all sat down around the circular kitchen table, just large enough for four.

"Well, not exactly expecting," Lifa said, tucking that stray lock of hair behind her ear. It promptly swung free again. "Bera has told us so much about you, though. We both reckoned we'd see you here at some point, to call on Bera."

"What has Bera told you about me?" I asked. I tried to keep my tone brightly conversational, but I couldn't help but feeling that things were about to take a dark turn. Something was very wrong here.

"Well, that she's been practicing her magic with you," Lifa said.

"She told you I've been teaching her magic?" I asked. What an odd lie to tell. As if I knew enough magic to teach a thing to anybody.

"No," Lifa said, trading a concerned glance with her husband. "No, she told us she was teaching *you* some things."

"We know you're born to be the volva, of course," Falr said. "But you've been away most of your life. You lost the traditions. Isn't that so?"

"True enough, so far as that goes," I said.

"So you're saying she *hasn't* been teaching you magic?" Lifa asked, and her eyebrows started to knit together in worry.

"No, and I'm not sure why she told you that," I said. "Hold on. I need just a minute."

I closed my eyes. I could feel them both watching me closely, which was distracting, but they both stayed silent. I controlled my breathing and then switched my perceptions until I was looking at the world through my magical eyes.

I could see the glow of life from the couple at the table with me, and another somewhere up above me. The cows made themselves felt, too, from the hillsides all around us.

But the only magical thing in that house was me. Of course I already knew she wasn't home, but if Bera had ever done any kind of spell inside this house, I would be able to sense the remnants of it. If it were an active spell like so many of the ones my grandmother left up to protect her mead hall, it would be even more clear to my eyes.

But there was nothing.

I opened my eyes and sucked in a breath, then took another drink of coffee. The coffee helped me feel grounded in the real world again.

Bera's parents were still watching me, searching my face for clues. It was maybe possible that Bera could do magic and just never did it here. But I was pretty sure if she had real power, I would feel vestiges of it inside her own home. She slept here, she ate here, this place was the focal point of her life.

No, I didn't think she actually did any real magic. But did she think she did, or did she knowingly tell her parents lies about it?

And if Bera was telling her parents lies like that, what else was she telling them? And where should I start questioning them about it?

"Is everything all right?" Lifa asked. "You were doing something there to check, weren't you?"

"Everything here is fine," I told her. Asking about the magic wasn't likely to lead to anything helpful. But what else might she be lying about? "Can I ask you two about Roarr?"

"Roarr?" Falr said with a frown. "What do you need to know about Roarr?" He exchanged a worried but confused glance with his wife.

"This is going to sound strange, but I need you to trust me," I said. They both nodded, anxious to help. "Can you just tell me everything you know about Roarr? Pretend I've just come into town and know absolutely nothing about him. What would you tell me?"

Falr looked to his wife and then deliberately took another sip of coffee, leaving the answer to her.

She told me absolutely everything about him, how he was an only child and a bit of an outsider even as a kid, how he had loved a girl from outside Villmark and then had lost her.

How he was even more of an outsider now, with the people of the village unsure if he could be trusted.

"No one knows if he was acting under the influence of a spell, or if he was helping Halldis of his own free will," she said as she wrapped up her tale. "I really think he might have been on the path to becoming a complete outcast, emotionally if not physically, were it not for Bera. She saved him." She gave me a warm smile, as if she was sure that I already knew all about this. That I must be asking about some other aspect of Roarr's life.

"What has Bera done?" I asked.

She gave me another confused look, confused but also troubled. Just by being here, I was making this pair question a lot of things they had been accepting as true. Finally, she said, "well, she's loved him. She's brought him back from despair. Surely you know?"

"She told you this, I'm guessing," I said. "Has Roarr been here to visit at all?"

"Well, no," Lifa admitted. "But how could Bera... I'm sorry, but it sounds like you're trying to say that Bera has been making things up, that she's been lying to us. But that just can't be true. I've seen the ring."

"What ring?" I asked.

"The engagement ring," Lifa said.

"It's been in his family for generations, that ring," Falr said. "I recognized it when she showed it to us. As a child I was a close friend of Roarr's father, Egil, and I remember his mother always wore that ring."

"Oh, dear," I said, and immediately regretted it when they both looked up at me with growing alarm. "I'm sorry. Roarr told me that someone had been sneaking into his house, even into his bedroom, to leave him messages. He didn't mention anything being stolen, though. And he thought it was Nefja, but now I wonder if he was just guessing. I really need to talk to Roarr."

"I don't understand," Lifa said. "You think Bera has been sneaking into Roarr's house?"

"I don't know," I admitted. "All I do know is that Roarr never gave her any ring. They are not engaged. I'm sorry; I'm afraid this is all a shock to you."

"That's putting it mildly," Falr said. "She kept telling us he'd come to call next week, always next week."

"We have to make her give that ring back," Lifa said.

"We'll sort everything out in time," I said. "But I have a few more questions that I have to ask you now."

"Of course," Falr said. He reached a hand across the kitchen table to hold on to Lifa's.

"The night before last, Nefja died. Did you know about this?" I asked.

They looked at each other but shook their heads.

"I know it doesn't seem like we're very far from town, but we don't head up that way much," Lifa said. "Bera even does the shopping for me. I haven't been into town in... months."

"Our son takes a lot of my wife's time," Falr said. "He was born a little different. He's nearly a teenager now, but in a lot of ways he's still a toddler."

"Most days he's an absolute dear," Lifa said a touch defensively. "But he has bad days."

"He can be violent," Falr said. "He doesn't mean to, but he lashes out. It's as much as Lifa and I can do to control him when he's going through his angry times."

"He keeps us tied to home," Lifa said. "That was getting tough on Bera, especially after she finished her schooling and had nowhere else to go. There was work enough to do around the farm, I could've used her help, but she needed an escape. That's why she started working with Ullr. Just to get out from here and be with other people her own age."

"She's a good girl," Falr said. "I don't understand why she's been lying to us, but I still know in my heart that she's a good girl."

"I understand," I said. I really wished I could stop pushing them to confront this new side to their daughter all at once, but I couldn't. I had to know what had happened to Nefja. "So Bera didn't tell you that someone had died? And she's your only outlet to news from in town?"

"I'm sure we would've heard it, eventually. The neighbors do stop by from time to time. But you have the gist of our situation," Falr said.

"Do you think it's significant? That she didn't tell us?" Lifa asked me.

"It might be," I said. "Nefja was also in love with Roarr. That might be the reason why she died."

"What are you saying?" Falr demanded, but I could see in his eyes he was already putting things together. "You think it was murder, this girl dying?"

"But Bera could never kill anyone," Lifa said, covering her mouth in horror. "No, it's not possible."

"How did Nefja die?" Falr asked.

"She fell into the well at the center of the village commons and struck her head on the ice," I said.

"No, definitely not Bera," Lifa said, sounding relieved. "How could she throw anyone down a well?"

"Well, and again I'm so sorry, but that does lead me to my next question," I said. "You believed that Bera was teaching me magic. Did you ever see this magic she said she could do?"

"It's not the sort of thing you can see," Falr said. His confused look was saying that I should know this better than he. But I had no idea what he thought magic even was. Or what it was that Bera thought she could do.

"Again, pretend I'm new to town and know nothing. Now, explain this magic to me."

"She can influence nature," Lifa said. "She has a way with animals. We noticed that in her at a very young age."

"With the cows?" I asked.

"With everything," Falr said. "Our dog, the goats, even wilder creatures like raccoons and possums. Everything comes when she calls. I've even seen a wolf eat out of her hand."

"And she told you that was what she was teaching me?" I asked.

"No," Lifa said. "She told me she was going to teach you moon magic."

"Moon magic?"

"She asks the moon for favors, and it grants them," Lifa said. "But she never tells me what she wished for, so I can't give you any evidence for that. But she's always out all night during the full moon. She's been doing that since she was little."

"The night before last, that was a full moon," I said. "Was she out all night?"

They looked to each other. Then they both nodded.

"I see," I said, but I wasn't happy. "She told me she came straight home from work. But if it was the full moon, then she didn't. Was she here where you could see her from the house? Do you know what she was doing?"

"No," Falr said. "When I went out in the morning to check on the cows, she was still gone from the night before. I'm certain of that; I walked past the open door of her bedroom and saw her empty bed myself."

"Where was she?" Lifa asked, although whether she was asking me, her husband, or the entire universe, I couldn't tell.

"We need to find her," Falr said. "She needs to answer some questions."

There was a sudden yowl from upstairs, a masculine voice that had the shrill alarm of a toddler's cries, but the deeper timber of an older boy, almost a man. Lifa leapt up and ran for the stairs without so much as a last look at me.

"It sounds like it's a bad day for your son," I said, and Falr nodded without speaking. "Help your wife with him. He needs you. I'll take care of Bera."

"What will you do?" he asked, his voice thick. "If she's hurt someone... even if she's just been breaking into houses and stealing..." He pressed a shaking hand over his eyes.

I got up from my chair and came around the table to put my arms around him as his body shook with sobs.

"Falr, I swear to you I'm going to do just what I said," I told him. "There is clearly something wrong with Bera. My only intention is to take care of her. Because she needs care. Do you understand?"

"I do," he said, and pulled himself together with a single inhalation of breath.

"I swear no harm will come to her," I said. "But I do need to find her. I'll send someone to let you know when I have her. All right?"

"Yes. Thank you," he said. I went back to the front door to get dressed for outside. After wiping his face on a clean dish towel, he came to open the door and see me out.

"I'll be back in any event," I said to him as I zipped up my parka. "I need to see what help you need with your son as well."

"Thank you, Ingrid Torfudottir," he said. "I know some are skeptical of you being our next volva. I'm ashamed to admit I was one of the most vocal on that score until today. I thought... but that doesn't matter now. I know you will do your grandmother proud. Your grandmother and all of your ancestors."

"I hope so. I certainly intend to try," I said.

Then I ran down the steps, then up the road, as quickly as my booted feet could take me through the drifts of snow.

CHAPTER TWENTY-FIVE

I JOGGED along the road as it skirted that low hill and had just reached the point furthest from either the house I'd just left and Loke's house still out of sight up ahead when something dark and furry darted into my path. I tried to pull up short but slipped on a patch of ice, then tumbled head first over the animal, which was furiously attacking my shins.

A loud snapping sound cracked through the air, and I really hoped that sound wasn't one of my bones breaking.

I sat up on my elbows, spitting out snow as I pushed my hat back out of my eyes. I crawled forward just enough to be sure that I might be bruised but wasn't actually hurt. Then I looked back at my feet to see that it was Mjolner who had tripped me.

"Mjolner!" I said. I had more choice words to follow, but before I had the chance to say them, there was another loud crack and a splintering of wood.

Only this time I saw what it was. A rock the size of a baseball had just impacted a fence post nearby with enough force to send shards of wood flying through the air.

And that fence post had another chunk freshly missing from its grayed wood surface, that one just a little further up.

If I had been standing, that first rock would've hit me square in the head. The second one had barely missed me after I fell.

And surely there was a third coming my way.

Trolls? In town? I knew they liked to throw rocks, but they also had a respect for me as a volva from when we had met before. I closed my eyes and, faster than I'd ever done before, I blinked myself to my magic awareness.

But there were no trolls anywhere around me. Just the dim light from the surrounding cows, the brighter light of a nonmagical human further up the road, and the blinding light from Mjolner who was moving to stand between me and that rock thrower.

I opened my eyes and tried to scramble back up to my feet, but the icy road kept slipping away beneath me. Then I felt an explosion of pain in my hip, like someone had just hit me with a baseball bat, right on the joint where all the bones met. The pain ran down my leg and echoed across my pelvis and I face-planted in the snow again.

Mjolner was meowing furiously at me, but for a moment all I could do was breathe. And even that breath came in jagged gasps. I didn't think I could move.

But I had to. Or that fourth rock was going to kill me.

I followed the sound of Mjolner's caterwauling and found him sitting atop a drift of snow. Then I realized it wasn't just a drift of snow, it was snow that had almost entirely buried an old stone wall that divided the cow pasture from the road.

With a fierce yell, I pushed myself up from the ground and tumbled over that wall to lie flat on my back, staring up at the gray sky just in time to see another rock sail over me. If I had been a half second slower, that rock would've picked me off the top of that wall.

Not that I was doing much better where I was. I knew from my peek into the magical world that the thrower was on the road between me and Loke's house. But they were closer now than they had been then, and I suspected that the thrower wasn't going to let this little wall get in their way.

As much as I had managed to roll over the wall when I absolutely had to, I still didn't think I had any running in me. Not with the throbbing pain in my hip. I was afraid something might be broken in there, but there was no way to be sure lying in the snow like I was. If I so much as sat up, my head would be a perfect target.

"Mjolner," I said. "You need to go get help. Find Thorbjorn. No, find Loke. He's probably closer. Just find anyone. And hurry!"

Mjolner came around to lean close to my face and lick my nose with his sandpaper tongue. Then he was gone, and I was alone.

"Bera!" I called out even as I tucked myself closer to the wall.

"Ingrid," Bera said, suddenly sitting atop the wall right over me. She had a rock in her hand, this one the size of a softball.

"Put the rock down, Bera," I said. I moved to sit up, but also to slide a little ways away from her.

She sneered at me. "Why?"

"Because I don't think you really want to hurt me," I said.

"How's the hip?" she asked, tossing and catching the rock on her palm.

"Point taken," I said through gritted teeth. The fact that she wanted to hurt me was indisputable. "But hurting me won't get you what you want."

"What do you know about what I want?" she said. "And don't speculate. I'm not so easy to understand as the other women in this town."

"You've been telling your parents a lot of stories that aren't true," I said. I had to shift my position to lean my right shoulder against the side of the wall, because sitting with even half my weight on my left hip was becoming unbearable.

"You see, that's where you went astray," Bera said darkly. "You never should've spoken to my parents. I can't let that go. You've meddled too far. You've ruined everything."

"I just wanted to figure out what happened to Nefja that night," I said. "If you just would've told me the truth before, I never would've had to talk to your parents. I know you were there that night."

"You know nothing," she said. Her mouth was trying to sneer at me again, but I saw a hint of fear in her eyes.

She didn't understand the first things about magic. But that might work to my advantage. She had no idea how much or how little I could actually do.

"Unlike you, I really can do magic," I said, putting as much of a bragging tone into my voice as I could. It wasn't easy when my teeth wanted to grit against the pain. "I know you were there. Tell me what happened."

"I was there *first*," she snapped. "Nefja shouldn't have been there. After all that ale, it shouldn't even have been possible for her to be there. But she was just determined to take everything from me, even things she didn't need at all!"

"I'm not following you," I said, shifting my position again. The pain was a constant throb, and it was more than a little hard to think.

"She was never going to have Roarr!" Bera shouted at me.

"Well, of course not," I said. "Roarr didn't want her."

"That wasn't going to matter," she said. "She was going to take him from me."

"How could she take him from you when you never had him either?" I asked.

"Don't be obtuse!" she shouted, hopping down from the wall to stand over me, that rock raised high like she was about to hurl it down at me.

Despite my bravest intentions, I flinched.

But then her mood switched again. My flinching had brought a quirk of a smile to the corner of her mouth, and she lowered the rock to resume gloating over me.

"I don't think you know anything about what happened that night," she said. "I don't think your magic works that way. I know you weren't there."

"Tell me what happened," I said. "I need to understand."

She looked at the rock in her hand as if seeking its advice. Then she closed her hand over it, hiding it from view within her thick mittens, and looked at me.

"I was there first," she said, calmer than before as she resumed her seat on the wall. "You know that well is older than the rest of the town. And it has very old magic associated with it."

"Go on," I said, shifting my position again. The dull throb of pain became a sharp stabbing before settling back down to a slightly more tolerable throb. My leg was going numb, and I really hoped that was from the cold snow soaking into my pants.

"I've read the oldest books, so I know things," she said with an arch air.

"Moon magic," I said.

"That's not in the books," she said. "I figured that out on my own. But what I've done is based on things I've read. I just transformed a few things into a more effective ritual."

"That's why you were at the well? To perform a ritual? It was a full moon, wasn't it?"

"It was," she said with a little nod. "More than that. It was the full moon closest to the winter solstice. That gives it extra power. And it was a clear night, not a cloud in the sky. So much had to line up just right, but it did! It was meant to be!"

"What was meant to be?" I asked.

"It was meant for me to look down into that well on that night and to see the reflection of the full moon above reflecting up at me from below. Don't you see? It all conjoins," she said.

"And what happens when you see that reflection?" I asked. "You get a wish?"

"More than a wish," she said with dripping disdain. "So much more than a wish. You can't wish for someone to be in love with you. That never happens. There are *rules*, as you well know. But seeing that reflection when the moon is centered just so over that well, that lets you cast the spell."

"To make Roarr love you," I guessed.

"To make Roarr realize that he already loved me," she snapped. "You can't create something from nothing. That's not how magic works. I would think that you of all people would know that."

"Well, I just started my lessons, you know," I said with an attempt at a self-deprecating laugh. The stab of pain from my hip jerked that into more of a gasp. When I had my breath back, I asked, "how did Nefja ruin it for you?"

"She interrupted," Bera said. "Some night while I was working she must have found my notebook, my most personal notebook with all my spells in it. She must have read it, then put it back. Because she knew what I was going to do, and she decided it should be her at that well at the appropriate hour."

"So she got herself out of bed to be there?" I asked.

"I guess so. I didn't see her approach. I was already there, watching for the moon to appear at the bottom of the well, when she just came up beside me and looked down into the well too."

"What did she say?" I asked.

"Nothing," Bera said with a shrug. "She just looked into the well and saw the moon wasn't centered yet. Then she leaned in further, like she could make it happen for her before it happened for me. She leaned in so far her feet were off the ground. And at the angle she was at, I knew she'd see the full face of the moon first. So I just... touched her shoulder."

"You touched her shoulder?" I repeated skeptically.

"I pushed her in. Just a little push, but that was it."

"You *killed* her," I said.

"Well, I regretted it," she said. "Her body broke the ice, and then there was no piece big enough to reflect the entire moon. But she wasn't sinking fast enough to leave me with a wide patch of water to reflect the moon either. I should've pushed her back out of the way, not into the well. I see that now. She probably would've hit her head on the cobblestones and knocked herself out. But at the moment, I just wanted her gone. You know?"

"No, I don't know," I said. "I've never wished anyone dead in my life."

"There's that word again. *Wish*," she said mockingly. "Do you really think wishing makes anything happen? No, if you want something to happen, you have to make it happen for yourself. I wanted Nefja gone, and now she's gone." She tossed the rock into the air and caught it, then raised it high again. "I want you gone now. So you're going to be gone."

"Wait!" I said, but she just cocked that rock back to throw it with all her force. I tried to scramble back, but everything had gone numb while I was sitting there, and I couldn't move that leg at all.

I threw my arms up over my head and waited for the blow to come.

Then there was a rush of noise, like the wind was racing up the road from behind me. I tried to turn to see, but the wall was in the way.

Then Bera yelped out loud as she was tackled off that wall to land hard in the snow. The rock flew away from her, skittering just past my foot without striking me.

Bera shrieked as she fought with whoever was still tangled up with her. Snow was flying everywhere, and I couldn't tell who was under that coat and hat. But whoever he was, he was desperately trying to catch her pummeling fists and pin her to the ground. She fought like she was possessed, screaming and flailing with inhuman strength.

But finally he succeeded, pinning both of Bera's arms under his knees as he sat on her chest. Her legs were still kicking and bucking, but she couldn't budge him.

Then he turned to me and pushed back his hat. "Ingrid. Are you all right?" he asked.

"Just fine, Roarr," I said.

Then I let my body flop back down onto the snow. I had only wanted to take some of the pressure of my weight off my hip, but instead my whole body just let go and the world drifted away from me for a single blissful moment without pain.

CHAPTER TWENTY-SIX

WHEN I CAME BACK to the world, I felt myself being gently lifted up off the ground.

"What happened?" I asked, looking around. There was no sign of Bera or of Mjolner. But the sun had moved quite a bit across the sky, and my whole body was aching with cold from lying on the snow.

"Bera is with her parents," Roarr said as he set me on a pile of furs.

"What's this?" I asked, trying to twist around to see what I was lying on, but the pain quickly had me lying still again.

"It's just a sled. I'm going to pull you to Falr's place for now. Your cat went to get the Thors and a wagon," he said.

"Mjolner told you that?" I asked.

"No, I told him that was what was required, and he just looked at me like he understood," Roarr said.

"He does that," I said.

Then Roarr picked up a rope that was tied to the two front corners of the sled and started pulling me over the snow, back to Falr's house. It was an old-fashioned sort of sled, built of wood on metal runners, and I made a point of keeping my arms folded over my chest so that I didn't lose any fingers.

"Mjolner brought you to help me," I said as I looked up at the sky. "He found you first?"

"I was actually not far away," he said over his shoulder as he continued pulling the sled. "I went out looking for you this morning since I hadn't heard from you. I found your note at your house and was just knocking at Loke's front door when Mjolner showed up out of nowhere and just started yowling at me. It felt like an emergency, so I followed him to you."

"Thanks," I said. "I think she was about to kill me."

"I'm sorry I didn't get there sooner and save you from getting hurt at all," he said.

"By the time I knew I was in danger, it was too late," I said. "Mjolner *did* try to warn me."

"He's a good cat," Roarr said.

"Apparently he trusts you," I said. "That means a lot in my book."

We had reached the bottom of the porch steps, and Roarr dropped the rope and turned back to face me.

"Do you want me to carry you again?" he asked.

"Let me give walking a go," I said. I held out my hands, and he took them, pulling me to my feet. I leaned up against him, my entire left side a throbbing mass of uselessness. But I could manage my right leg well enough to get up the stairs with his help.

My whole body was stiff from lying in the snow, and I'm sure I was lurching like a mummy still tightly wrapped, but I managed all the same.

Lifa was waiting with the door open and an anxious look on her face. The minute I was inside the house she slipped an arm around me so that I had support on both sides, and she and Roarr walked me over to the couch in front of the fireplace.

"I'm so sorry," she said. I just shook my head, waiting for the pain to subside before trying for words.

"Where is Bera?" Roarr asked, looking from Lifa to Falr, who had emerged from the kitchen to close the front door.

"She's in her room," Falr said. "Don't worry. She won't try to run away."

I wasn't so sure I wanted to bet on that, but there was little I could do about it in any event. I laid my head back against the couch, too tired to hold it up any longer.

"We're so sorry about all of this," Lifa said.

"We know now what happened to Nefja?" Roarr asked me. I nodded. "It was Bera?" he continued. I hesitated, all too aware of both of her parents watching me, but in the end I nodded again.

"We're so, so sorry," Lifa said miserably.

"I'm sorry too," Roarr said, taking her hands and guiding her to the chairs near the fireplace. He sat down in one and she sat in the other, her hands still clasped in his. "I had no idea that Bera felt this way. But that's no excuse. I knew Nefja did, and I did nothing about that."

"What do you think you could've done?" Lifa asked, sniffling.

"I should've been clearer to everyone about what I was feeling," he said. "My heart still belongs to Lisa. I think it always will. I should've said so, but given the circumstances, I just didn't want to talk about her to anyone. My grief is my own. But that isn't all of it. Mainly I didn't want to remind people of what I did."

"You were under a spell?" Lifa asked.

Roarr sat quietly, looking down at their clasped hands, for several long minutes. Then he gave the smallest of nods.

"Could Bera be under a spell as well?" Falr asked.

"I don't think so," Roarr said. "The only person who was using magic that way is gone now. I think we're all safe from that. Although Ingrid would know better than I."

"She has been contained," I said. "There is nothing magical about Bera, either coming from her or affecting her. I'm sure of that. But I'm also sure that something is wrong with her."

"Maybe this has been a growing problem for some time," Lifa said. "Maybe we've been too busy dealing with her brother to notice that she had problems too."

"What happens now?" Falr asked.

"The Thors are coming with a wagon," Roarr said. "They will bring Bera to the council. After that, I don't know."

"The council will decide," Lifa said with a little nod to herself. "We will abide by the council's decision."

There was a knock at the door behind me and then a bustle of motion as everyone else got up from their chairs at once. I closed my eyes just for a moment, and when I opened them again Thorbjorn was leaning over me, checking me over for injuries. Not that any were visible when I was still dressed for the cold.

"You bandaged your head," I said, gesturing at the gauze and tape neatly applied to his forehead.

"I did," he said as he looked up at me.

Then his oldest brother Thorulv was standing beside him. He had taken off his hat, and as he leaned close to me, I could see the barest fuzz of red hair growing through the blue of his tattoos.

"Is anything broken?" he asked.

"I don't know," I admitted. "I was walking on it a little bit before, so I think that's a no."

He frowned at my answer. "You need to have Brigida take a look at you. We're going to bring you back to town on the same wagon with Bera. Is that all right?"

"As long as you two are there, I'm sure it'll be fine," I said. "Where is she now?"

"Thorge and Thormund are bringing her down," he said. Then he stepped away from the couch and I was alone with Thorbjorn again.

"Are you sure you can you walk?"

"Just barely, with help," I said. "I got up the porch steps and over to the couch. I think that's pretty good, considering."

"Then nothing can be too badly broken," he said. "You're just bruised."

"That's your professional diagnosis?" I said. "I feel like I'm the one who was fighting frost giants, but it was just wee little Bera."

"Wee little Bera with a nasty pile of rocks," he said with a frown. "She had a stockpile. Right there on the side of the hill, just off the road. Like she knew she was going to need them."

I pushed myself up higher on the couch. "What is it?"

"Nothing," he said with a dismissive wave.

"No, something else is wrong. Not just Bera," I said.

"I can tell you later."

"Or you can tell me now," I pressed.

Thorbjorn sighed. Then he looked around the room as if to be sure no one was close enough to overhear. Then he leaned in close to whisper in my ear, "they weren't frost giants that my brothers and I were fighting."

"What were they?" I asked.

"Fire giants," he said. "They've never been so close to our borders before. It was like something was drawing them here. Something very strong. They were driven. Focused. They fought like crazy to get past us. Then, just like that, they stopped and went back to wherever they came from."

"What does that mean?" I asked.

"I don't know," he said. But I could tell in his eyes that whatever it was, it had him very worried.

I could now lay Nefja to rest, both physically and in my mind. I had learned what happened to her. Bera's fate was out of my hands, but that was actually a relief. I had no idea what could be done for her here in Villmark. In the world I had grown up in, she would surely have been deemed not sane to stand trial.

Things were different here, and what was considered a crime was different here. But everyone was one extended family in a way that wasn't possible where I had grown up.

The council would have to balance the needs of Nefja's families with the needs of Bera and her family. They would have to find a path to justice around all of that. I didn't envy them that work.

But this worry in Thorbjorn's eyes, for some reason deep in my bones, it felt like that was my worry too.

I just didn't know what I could do about it. At least, not yet.

CHAPTER TWENTY-SEVEN

WALKING in crutches on snow is no fun, in case you were wondering.

But I couldn't stay home until I was able to walk on my own. I gave myself a single night to rest up, but that was it.

I had missed one lesson with Haraldr already. I couldn't miss two.

So the morning after my injury I found myself bundled up against the deepening cold, my mittened hands curled around the crossbars of the very modern crutches that Nilda and Kara had scared up for me, making my way down the road that sloped down the hill from my house to the south end of town and Haraldr's house.

A flat road would've been easier. One with less ice, even better. But since I had no choice in the quality of the road, I just took it one ginger step at a time.

But I wasn't alone. Since I had first limped into my house after getting off the wagon the Thors had brought me home in, Mjolner had never let me out of his sight. He even sat on the edge of the bathtub as I had tried to soak the soreness out of my black and blue hip the night before.

Nothing was broken that wouldn't mend. But I felt bad for my little black cat. He seemed to be carrying a mountain of guilt around, even though he had saved me from that first, brain-smashing rock that likely would've killed me.

Nothing I said seemed to assuage that guilt of his. I really wished he *would* talk to me, like he always seemed just about to. But failing that, I could never know why he was so down. I could just make sure to get him a couple of cans of that tuna-flavored cat food he particularly liked and hoped that would buck his spirits up.

In the meantime, he walked beside me through the frigid cold. And when I climbed the steps up to Haraldr's front door one laborious step at a time, he stayed close by my side. As if he could catch me if I slipped.

I half expected him to wait outside as he usually did when I went somewhere in Villmark, but when Fulla let me in, he swished past my ankles to be sure he got inside.

Once more I followed Fulla down the long hallway, then waited as she knocked just once on the door before opening it to let me inside.

"Ah, Ingrid," Haraldr said from where he was building a small fire in his massive fireplace. "I see you're doing better."

"Than yesterday?" I asked, leaning on my right crutch as I lowered myself to my stool. I certainly didn't look better than I had the last time I had been in this library.

"Yes. You looked very gray at the council hall yesterday. But I see your color is back today," he said.

"How's Bera?" I asked.

"Brigida says she settled into her cell quietly enough," he said, turning his attention back to poking his fire.

"How long will she stay down there?" I asked.

"As long as it is necessary to keep the rest of the town safe," he said. "It's too soon to say yet if her troubles will pass or if she'll always be like she is. We haven't even diagnosed her yet."

"Who's going to do that?" I asked.

"We have people," he said.

"What sort of people?" I pressed.

He sighed, then turned away from the fire to sit on the stool across from mine. "This isn't common knowledge, but then again you aren't a common person. But maybe don't let it slip to Valki and Brigida that I've told you."

"Told me what?" I asked.

"We have people here who have left Villmark for a time, then returned," he said. "They tend not to mix with the others, and sometimes even their own families do not know that they have returned. They settle in secret apartments in the village, but more commonly they live alone in the woods or even further out towards the distant mountains. Usually it is someone who left to marry an outsider who returns when that relationship ended. But not always. Sometimes they come back for other reasons."

"What does that have to do with Bera?" I asked.

"One of these people who returned was what you call a psychiatrist," he said. "They had a practice out in your world. Bera is now their charge."

"So she's getting therapy?"

"And drugs too, if they will help. But that is even more secret. Not everyone appreciates the fact that this council allows trade with the outside world."

I nodded. That fact was clearer to me all the time.

But then another thought struck me. "Is Halldis getting therapy?" I asked.

He looked startled, but quickly recovered. "Enough such questions," he said brusquely. "How do you feel you are progressing in your studies?"

I knew he was changing the subject because he didn't want to answer my question. But was it because the answer was yes, or because it was no? Halldis had seemed all kinds of crazy to me. Shouldn't she also be given access to a psychiatrist? If she could be rehabilitated, weren't we obligated to try to rehabilitate her?

"Ingrid, how is it going with Fe?" Haraldr asked, bringing my train of thought to a crashing halt.

"Some progress, I think," I said. "Nothing like mastery, that's for sure."

"Ack! What is this talk of mastery? As if there is such a thing in magic," he said, throwing up his hands as if trying to disperse a cloud of gnats that were plaguing him. "Well, your grandmother did warn me."

"She did?" I asked. "When?"

"Before you came up here," he said dismissively. "Listen to me: you need to set aside your idea that mastery is something you should be striving for."

"It's important to have goals," I said defensively.

"Your goal is just progress," he said. "It's every day taking another step. You might look up and see the sun on the horizon before you, but I promise you you'll never get to it. But you can keep walking towards it, can't you?"

"I guess," I said. "So is it time to start working on the second rune?"

"Always in such a hurry," he said as if to himself. Then he leaned forward to look me straight in the eye. "No, it's not time yet."

"So my task is still trying to bond with Fe, then?"

"You don't think you've bonded with Fe?" he asked me, raising a single eyebrow questioningly.

"Did I?" I asked. I felt like there was something going on I didn't know about.

"You had a dream," he said leadingly.

"I did," I said. "I don't remember telling you about that."

"I don't have magic as you do, but I'm not totally without aware-ness," he said. "You dreamed of fire wyrms, didn't you?"

"Is that what they were?" I asked. "Like salamanders swimming through the bedrock. How is that even possible?"

"Your spirit self was cavorting with their spirit selves," he said. "You wanted to go where you aren't meant to go, and they were just going to bring you there. You got very close to finding yourself in a very sticky situation indeed."

"I did end up in a sticky situation," I said, shaking one of my crutches.

"And your cat saved you both times," he said. "You really are putting far too much pressure on that poor cat. Maybe think before you leap next time."

"The fire wryms were trying to trap me?" I asked, confused.

"No, they were doing your bidding," he said. "You feel prepared to face her, don't you? Halldis? I promise you that you are not."

"It wasn't exactly planned out," I said. "It just sort of happened. I felt something that I thought was her, and I wanted to investigate."

"In future when you have these thoughts, ignore them," he said.

"I don't think I can do that," I said. "I have to know."

"Then come to me first," he said. "And be careful what you draw to you. Your power is greater than you know, and you have precious little control over it."

"Wait a minute," I said, throwing up my hands. "Are you saying I brought the fire giants here as well?"

"There were fire giants?" he said. His shock seemed real. I slowly nodded.

"The Thors fought them off. Or they were fighting with them until the giants just gave up and left, apparently."

Haraldr got up from his stool and paced in front of the fire, hands folded at his back and head down as though his thoughts weighed it down.

"But wait," I said. "Thorbjorn left to face the giants the night before I had that dream. So never mind. I guess it was just a coincidence."

But my relief was short-lived, as Haraldr stopped pacing and spun to fix a look on me. "They were drawn by you all the same. The dream was your strongest call, but they felt stirrings the moment you first focused on Fe."

"But it never felt like I was even doing anything," I said. "Especially not before that dream. I felt like I was failing, over and over again."

"You weren't," he said firmly. "Your magic is stronger than you know. We must take greater care in future, you and I. At least your cat woke you from that dream. He saved us all."

I didn't know how to answer that. But then he walked over to stand over me and stab a finger at me. "You need to rely less on that cat of yours. There are limits even to his power."

"I didn't realize I was doing anything," I said. "I didn't know he was working so hard to protect me."

"No, I don't suppose you did," he said, his grave expression morphing to something friendlier in the blink of an eye. "There's so much work still ahead of us."

"Well, let's get started, then," I said, sitting up straighter on my stool. I wanted to look eager to work, but inside my heart was sinking lower and lower. I didn't think it showed, but the look in his eyes changed from stern teacher to compassionate guardian. He didn't know exactly what I was going through. He'd never done any of these things in anything but an academic sense.

But he understood my feelings all the same.

"No, not today," he said. He took my arm and helped me to my feet, then made sure I had a crutch tucked under each arm. "Follow me," he said, heading back out into the hall where Mjolner was waiting.

Mjolner looked me over as if assuring himself that I was still all right. Then he turned to follow Haraldr through the doorway to the kitchen.

I made my way after them at my own slower pace, struggling a little where the hallway had a step down into the kitchen. But there was no one there. I crossed the room to an open doorway that led into a sun-filled dining room.

The light from the rising sun was blinding, and at first I was only aware that someone else was in the room with Haraldr, Mjolner and I.

Then I was in that someone's arms, getting a tight hug. I knew those arms well. I knew that smell, too, of lefse and coffee and always slightly damp flannel.

"Mormor!" I cried, hugging her back even more tightly than she was hugging me. "You said you'd never make it here for breakfast time!"

"I make exceptions for near-death experiences," she said.

"I was never near death," I said. She pulled back to give me a deeply skeptical look. "Well, maybe a little. But only for, like, a split second. Mostly I was okay."

"It's been less than a week, Ingrid," she chided me. "I thought you'd start with something smaller than life-threatening danger."

"I know," I sighed. "But wait, I thought we were supposed to be kept apart from each other?" I looked around the room until I found Haraldr lingering near the doorway. "You specifically said she was a bad influence."

"So long as she doesn't attempt to teach you more magic, her influence should be... benign," he said. "Now, if you'll excuse me, I can't very well deny knowing the two of you were meeting clandestinely if I sit down and drink that tea with you."

"You're going to deny knowing we were meeting in your kitchen?" I asked.

"What's that? Didn't hear a thing," he said, then promptly left the room.

My grandmother and I sat down at the table loaded with more breakfast food than even the Thors could eat, but neither of us moved to touch it. She just smiled at me and said, "what did you want to ask me first?"

"How is everyone doing back in Runde, of course," I said.

"It's not even been a week, you know," she said. "Without you there, no one was solving crimes or chasing dangerous suspects through treacherous weather."

"So they don't even miss me yet," I said.

"Well, someone is missing his usual breakfast at my house since I'm not there," she said, glancing at her watch as if to confirm the time. "Which is just as well. When he stops by tomorrow, I'll actually have something to tell him."

"Andrew has been coming by?" I asked, my heart doing a little flip in my chest.

"Every morning, to see if I've heard from you," she said. "And a couple of more times a day just to check that I still haven't heard from you. Of course, those extra visits have pretenses attached to them. Very flimsy pretenses." Then she reached for the teapot and started pouring out two cups of steaming, lavender-scented tea. "Poor boy. I feel for him. It's hard being separated from those you care about."

"Tell me about it," I said gloomily. But he missed me. Even with how we parted, he still missed me.

I rested my chin on my hands and leaned in closer to my grandmother. "No, seriously. Tell me all about it. Every glorious, mundane detail. Don't leave out a single no-trolls-involved moment."

Her eyes flashed merrily at me and she put a few pieces of fruit on a plate before saying, "well, first of all, when I came down the hill after dropping you off here, he was already waiting for me, right there where the path ends at the bottom of the waterfall. Just to be sure I got back okay, he said."

"Of course he did," I said, reaching for a cinnamon roll. "And you thanked him for the gifts for me?"

"No, dear," she said. "Some things still need to be face to face between the parties involved."

I nodded, but to my surprise I didn't feel sad about this. There would be a wait, and I didn't know how long it would be, but I knew it had an end.

I would do everything in my power to make that wait as short as possible.

And if Haraldr was right, I had more than enough power to bend a few things to my will. They didn't all have to be bad things. I could draw good things towards myself too, I just knew it.

"Go on," I said to my grandmother. "Tell me how the café is doing."

As she talked, telling me what everyone had been up to in just a handful of days in such carefully chosen details it felt like I had been there for all of it, I felt a warm glow of confidence growing in my chest.

I would draw good things for Villmark, because it was my calling to strive for that. But I would draw good things for me and my friends as well. Because we, all of us, deserved good things.

And I was the one who could make that happen.

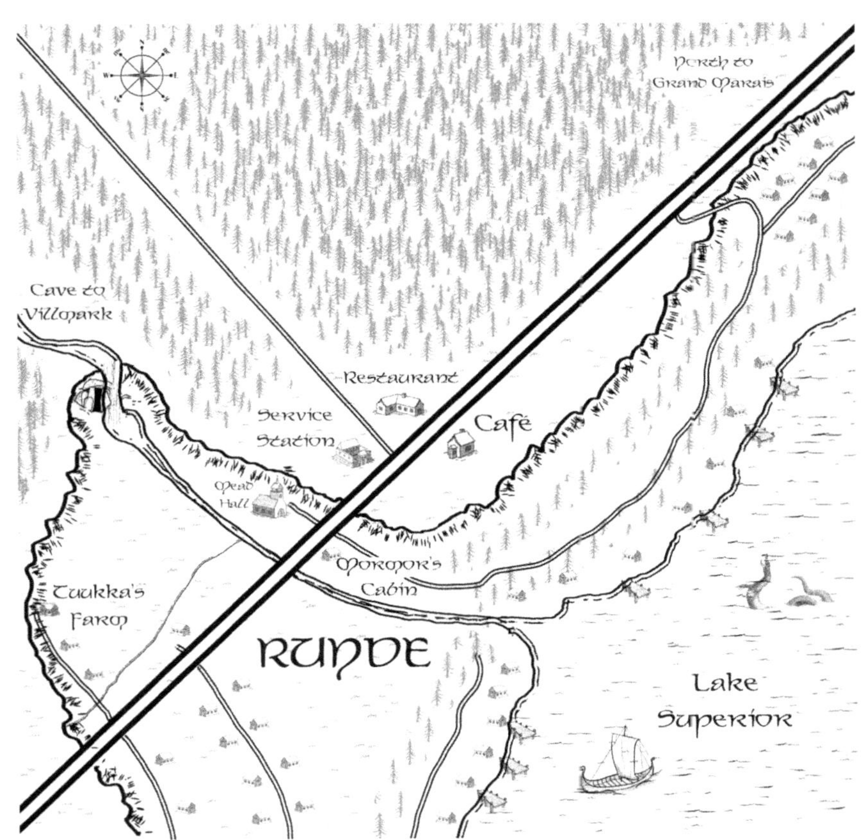

North to
Grand Marais
Cave to
Villmark
Restaurant
Service
Station
Café
Mead
Hall
Mormor's
Cabin
Tuukka's
Farm
RUNDE
Lake
Superior

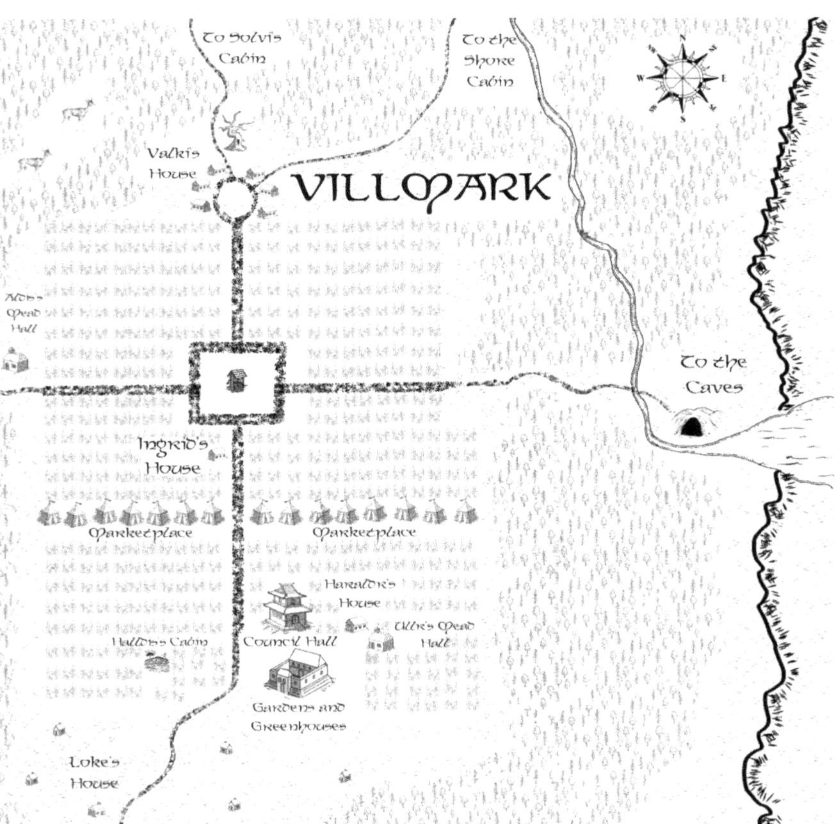

To Solvi's Cabin
To the Shore Cabin
N
W   E
S
VILLMARK
Valki's House
Aldi's Mead Hall
To the Caves
Ingrid's House
Marketplace
Marketplace
Harald's House
Haldis Cabin
Council Hall
Ulfr's Mead Hall
Gardens and Greenhouses
Loke's House

Bloodshed in the Forest, Book 5 in **The Viking Witch Mystery Series!**

THE WITCHES THREE
COZY MYSTERIES

In case you missed it, check out **Charm School**, the first book in the complete **Witches Three Cozy Mystery Series**!

Amanda Clarke thinks of herself as perfectly ordinary in every way. Just a small-town girl who serves breakfast all day in a little diner nestled next to the highway, nothing but dairy farms for miles around. She fits in there.

But then an old woman she never met dies, and Amanda was named in her will. Now Amanda packs a bag and heads to the big city, to Miss Zenobia Weekes' Charm School for Exceptional Young Ladies. And it's not in just any neighborhood. No, she finds herself on Summit Avenue in St. Paul, a street lined with gorgeous old houses, the former homes of lumber barons, railroad millionaires, even the writer F. Scott Fitzgerald. Why, Amanda can practically hear the jazz music still playing across the decades.

Scratch that. The music really, literally, still plays in the backyard of the charm school. Because the house stretches across time itself. Without a witch to protect this tear in the fabric of the world, anything can spill over. Like music.

Or like murder.

Charm School, the first book in the complete **Witches Three Cozy Mystery Series**!

204

THE WEAL & WOE BOOKSHOP WITCH MYSTERIES

In case you missed it, check out **The Teashop Terror**, the first book in the complete **Weal & Woe Bookshop Witch Mystery Series**!

No one knows more about every branch of magic than Tabitha Greene. She devoted years to studying the most esoteric texts, hunting down the most obscure source materials, and deciphering the most cryptic ancient scrolls. But her career in academia hits a dead end when no wizard will take her on as an apprentice.

Just because, despite being descended from two long and prestigious lines of witches, her attempts to actually perform any magic always fail. Often spectacularly.

But no more college means no more dorm life. And no magical skills means no real job skills, at least, not in the witchy world. And a life spent moving from school to school every few months was a life without real friendships. She finds herself alone with nowhere to go.

Then an uncle she barely remembers offers her a summer job, running his bookstore over the summer. The Weal and Woe Bookstore, located in a magical pocket world within a block of buildings just north of the old Mill District of Minneapolis, Minnesota.

Not exactly the pinnacle of all her hopes and dreams. But it's just for one summer, right?

Or so Tabitha tells herself. But unbeknownst to her, the Weal and Woe Bookstore is about to change her life.

The Teashop Terror, the first book in the complete **Weal & Woe Bookshop Witch Mystery Series**!

ALSO FROM RATATOSKR PRESS

The Ritchie and Fitz Sci-Fi Murder Mysteries starts with **Murder on the Intergalactic Railway**.

For Murdina Ritchie, acceptance at the Oymyakon Foreign Service Academy means one last chance at her dream of becoming a diplomat for the Union of Free Worlds. For Shackleton Fitz IV, it represents his last chance not to fail out of military service entirely.

Strange that fate should throw them together now, among the last group of students admitted after the start of the semester. They had once shared the strongest of friendships. But that all ended a long time ago.

But when an insufferable but politically important woman turns up murdered, the two agree to put their differences aside and work together to solve the case.

Because the murderer might strike again. But more importantly, solving a murder would just have to impress the dour colonel who clearly thinks neither of them belong at his academy.

Murder on the Intergalactic Railway, the first book in **The Ritchie**

and Fitz Sci-Fi Murder Mysteries, available everywhere books are sold.

FREE EBOOK!

Like exclusive, free content?

If you'd like to receive "A Collection of Witchy Prequels", a free collection of short story prequels to the Witches Three Cozy Mystery and Viking Witch Mystery series, as well as other free stories throughout the year, go to my website CateMartin.com to subscribe to my newsletter! This eBook is exclusively for newsletter subscribers and will never be sold in stores. Check it out!

ALSO BY CATE MARTIN

The Witches Three Cozy Mystery Series

Charm School

Work Like a Charm

Third Time is a Charm

Old World Charm

Charm his Pants Off

Charm Offensive

The Witches Three Cozy Mysteries Books 1-3

The Witches Three Cozy Mysteries Books 4-6

The Viking Witch Mystery Series

Body at the Crossroads

Death Under the Bridge

Murder on the Lake

Killing in the Village Commons

Bloodshed in the Forest

Corpse in the Mead Hall

Slaying on the Lake Shore

Bones by the Forest Road

Sacrifice Behind the Falls

Body Under the Café

Assassination in the Glade

Bewitchment After the Storm

Predator in the Lanes

Threat From the North

Snare in the Blind Alley

Ashes Beneath the Tree (available July 14, 2026 direct from me or August 11, 2026 in stores everywhere)

The Viking Witch Mysteries Books 1-3

The Viking Witch Mysteries Books 4-6

The Viking Witch Mysteries Books 7-9

The Weal & Woe Bookshop Witch Mystery Series

The Teashop Terror

The Salon & Spa Scandal

The Bookseller Blunder

The Entrepreneur Enigma

The Novelty Shop Nightmare

The Courtyard Conundrum

Short Story Collections

Bubbly, Bicycles and Brides

The Dorothy Lundegaard Mysteries

Fruitcake, Festivities and Firelight